TOM MALONE

Captured

To Isaiah

For all evils there are two remedies - time and silence.

ALEXANDRE DUMAS

Prologue

They walked silently. The sound of their shoes echoed off the houses that lined the narrow street. There was no need to speak. They knew the plan.

As they moved down 40th Avenue, they saw a couple dressed in fine evening attire cross the street into the light, looking cautiously over their shoulders as they moved. The woman wore a dazzling dress and a jeweled headband, while the man wore a tailored suit with a wide-brimmed fedora.

"We must be in the right neighborhood," Patrick said.

The couple disappeared into an alleyway.

"There it is," Patrick said.

Michael and Patrick turned into the alleyway, passing rickety wooden fences as they walked. They came to a driveway that led to a house's side door. Patrick hesitated, looking at Michael for reassurance. With a nod from his cousin, Patrick knocked on the door. A slot slid open, revealing a pair of eyes.

"Who are you here to see?" a deep voice said through the door.

"We're here to see the Czar," Michael said.

"The Czar is dead," the voice said.

Michael felt his nerves fire in his legs. He was ready to run if the next phase of the password didn't work. Taking a deep breath, he continued.

"Long live the revolution," Michael said.

The slot slammed shut. Michael looked at Patrick, unsure if the password had worked.

Then, a series of locks clanked and unbolted, and the door swung open. Michael and Patrick entered the dark opening. The guard slammed the door shut behind them, locking it, trapping any retreat. They walked nervously down a dark staircase. The wooden steps creaked underneath their feet. They reached the bottom of the staircase, landing firmly on cracked cement. A black door blocked their progress. Michael looked to Patrick, unsure whether or not he should open the door. Turning back was not an option, so he turned the doorknob.

Chapter 1

Sweat poured from Michael Sullivan's face, dripping down his beard. He gripped the wooden axe handle and raised it above his shoulders. Pulling with strained muscles, he chopped into the tree. Wood splinters exploded outward from the force of the blade, digging into Michael's exposed forearms beneath his rolled-up flannel sleeves. His shoulder was starting to lose its strength; the humidity and cold rain drained his energy this late in the day.

As soon he pulled his axe blade from the thick evergreen trunk, another axe blade hacked into the tree. This back-and-forth combat between dueling axes and the defenseless tree trunk produced a rhythm; birds chirping and singing in the forest provided the melody.

About 30 men filled this part of the forest. Each one chopped with axes or sawed in pairs. Some even hoisted themselves high into the canopy to cut limbs and prepare the way for the fall. The silence of hard work was only interrupted by warning shouts and the grunts of muscle fatigue.

"Timber!" Michael shouted, quickly removing his axe from the tree trunk.

Loud cracks echoed through the pine tree forest. Branches snapped. The healthy tree trunk popped as it fell. Men scattered, pushing each other out of the way to avoid certain death.

Michael smiled, wiping his forehead with a rag from his back pocket. He scrubbed wood chips from his beard, which had grown long after more than a month in the Oregon wilderness.

Edward Bishop slapped Michael on the shoulder. He carried a pristine demeanor despite the rugged environment, especially compared to Michael's grizzled appearance.

"How many trees is that for you today," Edward asked.

Michael squinted as he smiled, creating creases around his eyes. His teeth gleamed through his beard.

"I love it out here," he said. "Hard work. Nature. And good company."

Edward threw his head back and laughed, feigning modesty.

"Come on, Sullivan," Edward said, "let's call it a day."

"Daylight is almost gone, I suppose," Michael said.

He walked with Edward and a few other loggers through the dense forest undergrowth for a mile before they reached the logging outfit's basecamp. The walk was quiet; the men were exhausted.

When Michael reached his tent, relief overcame him. It wasn't much, but it was home, no matter how temporary. He ducked under the tent flap and dusted off his axe with a rag, as he did every evening. He placed his axe on a short table that held all of his worldly possessions: a journal, a billfold, and a Bible. A newspaper sprawled on his bed, displaying headlines from the war in Europe; it seemed like the Kaiser's German army was pushing forward on the Western Front. It also mentioned something about the Bolsheviks gaining traction in Russia. A long way from the Oregon wilderness, as far as Michael was concerned.

Michael's joints moved stiffly as he removed his leather gloves. He tossed them onto his cot next to yesterday's newspaper.

"Hey, Sully," Edward shouted, "dinner's almost out."

"Thanks, Eddy," Michael replied. "I'm on my way."

Michael grabbed his jacket and threw it over his thick flannel shirt. Since the business of chopping down trees was physically demanding, he only wore a flannel shirt into the forest each day, no matter the temperature. But at night, when the sun set and the spring chill picked up in the forest, he needed his wool-lined canvas jacket. His black beard hung so low that it provided enough warmth for his face, but he decided to wear a knit cap to ward off the chill further.

As he stepped out of his own tent, he saw Edward waiting for him. Edward's sport coat looked like something out of the English countryside. Michael never understood why Edward paid so much attention to style; he worked in the forest. Edward placed a brown fedora on his head with a feather that matched his sport coat. He had changed into shoes that would fit an estate owner's lifestyle. Michael thought Edward had shaved, but it was hard to tell because Edward shaved every morning.

"You know we eat dinner with a bunch of grumpy, grizzly old men every night," Michael said. "There aren't any ladies around to impress."

"I don't see the need to compromise my style," Edward said. "Even if we are in the wilderness."

They laughed and started the short walk to the dining tent. A consistent drizzle coated the ground, creating soft mud that stuck to Michael's work boots. Edward avoided the growing number of puddles with precision. The scent of fresh pine filled their lungs, followed shortly by the smell of boiled potatoes.

Dozens of men flocked to tables underneath a canvas dining tent, which hung between eight trees. The dense pines shaded the ground enough, but the canvas tent provided some reminiscence of civilization to the otherwise primeval forest. Michael grabbed his potato, filled his bowl with porridge, and grabbed his water ration. He found an empty section on a long wooden table and sat down. Edward sat in an empty seat across from him.

Edward grabbed his fork eloquently. His upbringing hadn't escaped him, even in the wilderness. His white arm paled in the waning sunlight. Michael always wondered how Edward's arms stayed so pale when he worked outside all day. Though Michael had white arms, his skin freckled and tanned in the occasional sunlight that the Cascade Range produced, giving his forearms the appearance of having been exposed to the elements during his lifetime.

More men filed in with their meals, sitting with the same group they always sat with, eating the same food they always ate, arguing over the same topics they always discussed. Sometimes, those arguments turned into brawls or fistfights, but nothing major ever came of the feuds.

Michael tore off a piece of bread and chewed it quickly, talking as he chomped. Edward watched with amusement as he cut his potato into precise slices.

A grizzled logger walked into the dining tent. His scraggly beard hung over his thick, flannel overshirt. As the man stood in line, he saw Michael. His eyes, simmering with anger, fixated on Michael's bread, and then on Michael himself. Sensing someone staring at him, Michael lifted his eyes from his plate and found the grizzled logger's gaze.

Last week, the grizzled logger had taken the last piece of bread. Michael threw a slick remark his way, causing the grizzled logger to push Michael, who returned the push with a swift punch to the jaw. The man tackled Michael to the ground. Soon enough, the two were engaged in a brawl in the dirt. A few men pulled the fight apart, and everyone returned to their meal.

But the grizzled logger hadn't forgotten. His jaw still carried a bruise from Michael's punch. Michael's ribs still felt sore, but he knew he had the upper hand. So, he stared at the grizzled logger, forcing him to break his eye contact.

Smiling, Michael returned his focus to his dinner plate. More men from the forest trickled into the tent and filled their usual spots around the tables. A few new faces appeared, while some old faces were quietly absent. There were always people moving out, and new people always filled their spots.

Michael was used to this routine. He had been a logger since he left secondary school a few years earlier. He moved from his dilapidated tenement in North Portland, where he grew up with siblings and cousins. And a whole clan of other Irish immigrants. And a wave of Black families from the South who came to work in the shipyards. It was the only neighborhood they could live in. They couldn't buy, of course. And rent continued to rise. And the living quarters were close. But at least the conditions cultivated a close community.

The Sullivans lived on the third floor. The roof leaked. Mice shared their walls, and sometimes their pantry, which was usually empty, anyway. Michael's father worked in the shipyards on the shores of the Willamette River. His mother died in childbirth. He never talked about it, and he didn't let anyone else talk about his mother, either. Michael was a middle child. His older brothers helped guide him into secondary school, but after that, he was on his own. The older siblings found street gangs to protect them. Or they moved away. Or they found prison. Michael wasn't sure anymore, but all options seemed possible.

Aside from his cousin, Patrick, Michael didn't have much support to lean on. And Patrick wasn't exactly an upstanding citizen. The Sullivan cousins got into their share of fistfights at school and around the neighborhood, but the fights always carried with them a sense of justice, at least in Michael's mind. It was always someone making a derogatory remark about the Irish or his cousin that set him off. But the most notorious spark came from rudeness to women. Michael found a deep level of fury when a kid from a few blocks away heckled the girls in his tenement, or made a comment about his mother.

When Michael decided to move out of the city and into the forest, his cousin called him crazy. He didn't mind. He knew that if he stayed in the city, it would be difficult to maintain his sense of morality while striving to get out of the trap of poverty. The reality of poverty could overtake his sense of pure ethics, and he wanted to do everything in his power to be the person his mother wanted him to be: honest, hard-working, respectful, and joyful.

But the city would change that. He had seen his older brothers begin their fall from morality as soon as they became caretakers. Sure, they worked honest jobs during the day, but nighttime provided lucrative opportunities.

Michael needed to avoid his own downfall. He had some schooling, but he wasn't well-trained in reading, writing, or mathematics. And this hindered his ability to leave. But he did have street sense and the courage to make a move. He also had some intangible societal advantages that some people in his neighborhood didn't have. He got in contact with a logging outfit that harvested old growth timber in the Coastal Range, far enough away from the city for him to spend his hard-earned money.

But the forest was foreign to Michael. His street smarts didn't help him out here. He needed survival skills. Ancient knowledge that the first humans used to navigate their lives. He lacked that knowledge. At first, anyway. It grew with time and experience.

And of course, there was Emma. She grew up in a neighborhood just across the bridge from Michael's tenement. He met her in secondary school and immediately knew he wanted to marry her. She was kind, intelligent, and beautiful. And she made Michael happy. After secondary school, Emma had plans to become a schoolteacher herself, but he knew he wouldn't be able to provide for her. At least not right away. He needed to work his way toward earning her as a companion. But the spark was there.

So, Michael moved to the forest, where he chopped timber as a low-level worker. He earned one free weekend each month and he spent it kindling his love for Emma in the city before he returned to the wilderness to earn enough money to contribute to a marriage.

He loved her with all his heart, and she was the only woman he had ever loved. Emma was charming, but she was no pushover. She stuck up for herself, even to Michael when he said something patronizing. She had changed him somehow. He couldn't pinpoint it, but he knew this change was positive. And he knew he wanted to be with her forever. But he couldn't enter into a marriage without something monetary to contribute. Her father would never allow it.

On his first day in the forest, he met Edward; he saved Michael from nearly chopping his own hand off. Since then, Michael and Edward had become more like brothers. Edward worked in the forest for a year before Michael arrived. And somehow, Michael had become Edward's supervisor, though Michael didn't pay much attention to a title. They shared stories, looked out for each other, and fought occasionally, just like brothers.

Edward came from Portland's West Side. He was born to a wealthy family, but his family lost most of their fortune through some bad investments. Edward's mother always spoke about the Bishop legacy, instilling in her son the necessity to maintain a dignified image. His father pressed the endurance of the Bishop line. He often spoke to his son about the Bishop's family legacy, descended from English royalty many centuries ago. Edward doubted the historical validity of this legacy, but it fueled his drive to maintain familial honor.

As a teenager, his ego crashed along with his family's prestige; the future he felt entitled to was no longer possible. Edward planned to enlist and join the Great War in Europe. Naturally, he would enter the army as an officer, which would enhance his status above those dogs in the trenches. But when he finally became old enough to enlist, the descriptions of trench warfare had terrified him.

Adjusting his plans, he had no choice but to leave and find work. His parents' downtown connections no longer carried weight; the Bishop family had fallen out of fashion. But he knew the forest held wealth in its resources. By watching his fellow loggers, Edward learned to work smarter, not harder.

And Edward knew that by working smarter, he could regain the status he thought he deserved.

He started small, testing his new mentality against the dull minds in the forest. He placed occasional wagers on sure bets. He planted seeds of power, making connections with loggers from families with some form of prestige. He used his meager paycheck to purchase influence within the logging outfit, but he had recently started expanding his scope.

"You know," Edward said, placing his fork down precisely on his plate.

"What is it, Eddy?" Michael asked.

"I see all these loggers that look like they're 60 years old," Edward continued. "But I know they're only about 22, somewhere around our age."

Michael took a large bite from his potato and nodded, encouraging Edward to continue.

"They've worked out here for so long, and in such hard conditions. It's wearing on their health. Their lifespan."

Michael raised an eyebrow and chomped on his potato.

"What does it matter?" Michael asked.

"I don't want to be one of those men who works myself to death in the forest," Edward said. "There has to be a faster method to advance in the world. Especially coming from a family like mine."

Michael gulped his water, exhausted from the day's work.

"Don't you have grander aspirations than working in the forest your whole life?" Edward asked.

"Of course, I do," Michael said. "Someday, I'll marry Emma and we'll settle down on a small farm somewhere just outside the city. Maybe we'll even have a few children. I'll spend Sundays reading on the deck with Emma, while the kids play in the yard."

"Grand ambitions, my friend," Edward said. "When do you plan on enacting that plan?"

Michael reached into his jacket pocket and held the box securely. He had saved for nearly four months to afford the small ring inside. He removed the box and placed it on the table.

"Is that an engagement ring?" Edward asked. "When are you going to ask her to marry you?"

"I don't know, really," Michael said. "Next time I'm in Portland, I suppose."

"Well, when is that going to be?" Edward asked.

"I haven't decided," Michael said. "I'm nervous to ask her."

Edward slapped the table. Michael's fork bounded from his plate. Loggers from the other end of the table grunted and looked in Edward's direction. He didn't care. This could be the moment Edward needed to enact his ambition.

"Emma is a schoolteacher," Edward said. "It's Friday. Let's head into Portland early tomorrow morning, have a Saturday night on the town, and you can propose on Sunday."

Michael fiddled with the box. His nerves seemed to prevent any form of an answer.

"Come on, chap," Edward said. "You've got no time to waste."

"Alright," Michael said. "But I don't know about having a night on the town."

Edward smirked, knowing he could convince Michael to have a few drinks tomorrow night. Even with a strong constitution, Michael was easily persuadable.

"We'll figure that out later," Edward said. "Let's focus on getting you to Portland for the proposal. Let the spring of 1918 be remembered as the moment when your entire life changed."

Edward reached across the table and slapped Michael on the shoulder. They stood and cleaned their plates, placing them in the tray for another day's use. As they stepped out from underneath the dining tent, Michael noticed that the rain had stopped, or at least lightened up.

The walk back to camp was short, just a few hundred feet. They walked along the well-worn mud path as the sun faded behind the hills. Edward cautiously sidestepped the mud puddles in his expensive shoes; Michael stomped right through them.

"Mail's here!" a logger shouted near the tents.

Heads poked out of tents, hoping to receive letters from loved ones in the city.

"This one's for you, Sullivan," the logger said.

"Anything for me?" Edward asked.

The logger flipped through the small batch of envelopes and nodded his head. He handed a small envelope to Edward, whose lips curled into a smile.

"Who is your letter from?" Michael asked.

Covering the return address on the envelope, Edward quickly stashed the letter in his pocket.

"No one," Edward said. "Just a business associate in the city."

Edward didn't want Michael to grow suspicious, so he shifted the conversation.

"Who's your letter from, Sully?" Edward asked.

Michael beamed. His face flushed slightly just holding the letter.

"It's from Emma," Michael said. "Her letters always fill me with such joy."

"I suppose they would," Edward said.

Michael nodded. He used a small knife to open the letter. Angling the paper, he caught more light from the rising moon. A small tear trickled from his eye, and his smile never faded.

Edward leaned against a tree, watching Michael's reaction, wishing he could receive a letter that would move him to such joy. Instead, the letter in his own pocket tore at his conscience.

"I remember when you first introduced me to Emma a few years back," Edward said.

Michael looked up from his letter, fixing his memory on that evening in Portland.

"It wasn't certain whether she would go for you or for me," Michael said, smiling.

Edward forced a light-hearted chuckle, masking his disappointment. His guilt about his own letter began to fade.

"She was always going to end up with you," Edward said. "It's that damn Irish accent you inherited from your father."

Michael laughed, waving his hand to shove off the notion.

"Well, I'm going to turn in," Michael said. "I'll see you in the morning. We can catch an early ride from a shipment going into town."

Edward continued to lean against the tree. He saw a flickering candlelight illuminate Michael's tent, where he undoubtedly sat rereading Emma's letter. The moon created shadows through the massive pine trees in the silent forest. Edward sunk into the shadows; his green eyes glowed in the moonlight.

The Bishop legacy will rise again, he thought.

Chapter 2

A light spring rain fell as Michael and Edward dashed along Second Avenue. Street lights illuminated the bustling city. Cars moved slowly down the road, splashing through puddles as they drove. People flooded the sidewalks in their evening attire. Saturday night buzzed through the bars and shops, up and down alleyways and main streets.

Michael wore his grey newsboy cap that matched his grey three-piece suit. It was the only suit he owned. He had saved his logging wages for an entire month to buy it; he wanted to look presentable when he proposed to Emma.

Edward's brown fedora contrasted with his blue suit. It was a bit older than he would have liked, a relic from a time when his family had wealth and status. He knew that one day soon, he could buy new suits from the finest tailors in the city. But he had to be patient. Calculated.

He had burned the letter he received yesterday, but its implications excited Edward. This was the opportunity he needed to restore his family's status.

They passed restaurants, bars, and coffee houses that sat underneath upscale apartments and flats. Fire escapes wound through alleyways, hiding just out of sight in the shadows. A few horses trotted through the streets, surpassed by the newer Model T from Ford. Cigar smoke lingered in the air. The smell of the sewer rose from the underground.

As the rain subsided, Michael and Edward walked toward the edge of the sidewalk, away from the awnings that offered some protection from the evening mist.

"Emma lives just down the road on Third and Morrison," Michael said. "I want to go there now and get the proposal out of the way."

Edward's eyes shifted nervously at the suggestion.

"No, let's wait until tomorrow," Edward said. "We need to celebrate your last night as a free man."

Michael pulled his cap over his face temporarily, hiding his excitement over marrying the love of his life. He couldn't wait to propose. He couldn't wait to get married. But he didn't want to look like he'd gone soft, either. Whether he would admit it or not, Michael cared about Edward's perception of him. The social power of acceptance from the upper class plagued Michael's esteem.

"You know you'll be my best man, right?" Michael said.

"Really?" Edward said. "Even over your brothers?"

"I haven't seen them in years," Michael said. "I'm sure they're in jail, or barricaded somewhere in the tenements on the other side of the river."

Edward smirked, but his heart sank.

"Well, I'd be honored to be your best man," Edward said.

He wrangled Michael into a headlock as they walked along the cobblestone. They ducked into a bar to grab a drink. The lights were dim. Uneven floorboards guided the men to the dark wood bar top. A bartender stood behind it cleaning pint glasses, his sleeves rolled up above his elbows. A drummer and a trumpet player created quiet music in the corner of the bar on a stage. Edward flashed his wallet to the bartender to grab his attention.

"Two whiskeys, old chap," Edward said. "We want to start the night off right."

The bartender nodded and grabbed a bottle of brown liquor from the back shelf. He poured quickly and placed two whiskey glasses in front of the men. Michael reached for his wallet to pay for the drinks, but Edwards waved his hand away.

"It's your last night as a free man," Edward said. "I'm buying your drinks all night."

Michael tipped his hat to Edward in appreciation. They raised their glasses and sipped their drinks before heading to a small wooden table near the middle of the narrow room. A few other tables were full, but there weren't many tables in the bar to begin with. Edward watched the drummer play his rhythm with precision.

"Is this liquor hitting you yet, Eddy?" Michael asked.

"Not quite," Edward said. "Maybe we should order a round of tequila to speed things up."

Michael shook his head in dramatic protest.

"Next thing you know, we'll be headed down to Mexico to fight with Pancho Villa," Michael said.

Edward smiled and leaned back in his chair. After watching the drummer navigate thee drum set for a bit longer, he leaned his weight back onto the table and fixed his eyes on Michael's glass.

"What do you love about Emma?" Edward asked. "What makes you want to marry her?"

"Everything about her, Eddy," Michael said. "Her intelligence is far greater than my brain can ever attain. Her kindness and

17

generosity inspire me. She has the courage to work for a living rather than simply depend on a husband to fund her life. She comes from a loving family of humble means. She's beautiful without trying. And I know she will be an incredible mother one day."

Edward nodded with narrow eyes as he listened to Michael's reply. The drummer's beat slowed while the trumpet player reached a higher octave.

"She is a fine woman," Edward said quietly.

Michael nodded in obvious agreement. He grabbed his glass and gulped down his whiskey, slamming his glass on the table.

"Another round, Sully?" Edward asked.

"I can't drink too much tonight, Eddy," Michael said. "I have to make it to church tomorrow morning."

Edward smiled and rolled his eyes.

"You Irish Catholics are always so concerned about going to church," Edward said. "You pious lad."

Michael feigned a reverent bow.

"Well, I'm going to head to the restroom," Michael said.

He stood and disappeared toward the back of the bar. Edward sat alone, watching other customers enjoy the company of the people at their tables. He felt slightly out of place in such a dingy establishment. Sure, he was in a trendy part of the city, but this was not the type of place his family usually frequented. At least, they never used to before they lost their fortune.

Edward remembered the lavish dinner parties his family hosted at their manor in the hills. Logging in the forest was an escape from the reality that his last name didn't matter anymore in the city of Portland. He loved the wilderness; he could live a simple life. But instilled ambition to succeed overcame his desire to live simply. And so, he found himself in a dark bar sipping whiskey from half-cleaned glassware.

Michael emerged from the darkness and stood next to the table.

"I can't believe this place has a telephone," Michael said. "I asked the bartender to use it. I phoned Emma's building. She and a friend are going to meet us in 30 minutes a few blocks from here at a bar near their building."

Edward raised an eyebrow at Michael's idea. His pulse increased.

This could ruin everything, Edward thought. *And I'll have to see her with him*.

"But don't worry, Eddy," Michael said. "I'm not going to propose tonight. I have the ring in my pocket, but I promise I'll wait until tomorrow when the time is right."

Edward rolled his eyes discreetly. He stood, pushed in his chair, and placed his fedora on his head. They walked into the city, greeted by a slight chill. Michael pulled his jacket across his body and buttoned it up, pulling his collar closer to his neck beneath his beard.

They walked into another bar. This one was well-lit, a stark contrast to the first bar. The elegant red leather booths and gold-rimmed railings provided a sense of sophistication that Edward was accustomed to. It was one of the fanciest places Michael had ever seen. He knew he couldn't afford much in a joint like this; he felt out of place, uncomfortable.

People filled the room in their distinguished dresses and finely tailored suits. Michael saw an empty booth in the back of the bar, so he snagged it before another group could. A server appeared, dressed in a black-and-white tuxedo.

"What can I get for you gentlemen this evening?" he asked.

"We're actually waiting for two more in our party," Michael

said.

"But we'll take two whiskeys while we wait," Edward said.

He handed cash to the server, who took it with gratitude. Edward insisted that he purchase Michael's drinks for the evening, even though he had little money to his name. Providing the appearance of wealth was almost more important than actually having money. Plus, Edward knew his wealth would appear soon enough. If things unfolded according to plan, his wealth would increase by the end of the night.

As the two men sipped their whiskey, Emma and her friend walked through the crowd. Michael stood and waved calmly, trying his best to hide his boyish excitement.

Emma's beauty illuminated from within the crowd. Her gentle nature and quiet confidence forced people to provide a path for her, watching her as she moved gracefully to Michael's table. Blonde hair rested in a long braid on her shoulder, shaded by her red brimmed hat. Her red dress floated along the floor. As she approached the table, she removed her overcoat; the server appeared promptly to take it from her. Michael and Edward stood to greet Emma and her friend.

"Good evening, gentlemen," Emma said. "This is my neighbor, Audrey. She lives in the flat next to mine."

Emma nodded toward Edward, hoping that he would take an immediate interest in Audrey. Edward once confessed his interest in Emma, and being around him still made her feel uneasy, especially in front of Michael.

Michael sat across the booth from Emma. His left hand grasped the ring box in his jacket pocket; he knew he couldn't propose tonight, but the excitement controlled him. He smiled sheepishly at her, and she returned the smile.

Emma knew Michael was her soulmate, the man she wanted

to marry, the man she wanted to raise a family with. Her father, on the other hand, wasn't convinced. Emma came from a Protestant family with some money. Marrying a Catholic from the tenements wasn't her father's idea of a suitable arrangement for his daughter. Michael knew this; Emma's father was a blunt man. So, Michael spent most of his time trying to win her father's approval while maintaining an honest sense of self. But no matter what he did, the implication of being a poor, Irish Catholic still established a barrier for Emma's father.

But that was Michael's identity. It was the culture and environment that he was born into, and it was this upbringing that shaped him into the man he had become. He was proud to be Irish, proud to be Catholic, and, most importantly, proud that he had found a person like Emma to share his life with.

A few years ago, a father's approval would have stopped him from moving along with his own life. However, after spending so much time in the forest under dangerous circumstances, Michael had found some courage, a feature he tended to shy away from as a kid. Now, Michael didn't care about her father's approval. All he needed was Emma's affection. She was a strong, independent woman. If she wanted to marry Michael, she would, regardless of her father's concerns.

"It's nice that you boys came into the city for the weekend," Emma said. "I can't believe it has been a month since I've seen you, Michael."

"It has been far too long, my dear," Michael said. "I'm grateful that you write to me every week. It keeps me going out there in the woods."

Emma blushed. She wanted to reach across the table and hold Michael's hand, but she knew an action like that was frowned upon in public, especially between a non-married couple.

"I do love you, you know," Michael said.

"My dear, I know you do," Emma said. "And you know that I love you madly."

Audrey eyed Edward from across the table, wishing he could say something romantic to her. She admired his precise style of dress and his angular facial features. She wondered if he was honest and simple like Michael. Audrey batted her eyelashes at Edward, but he didn't notice. He was looking at Emma.

Chapter 3

Michael stood next to the booth and grabbed Emma's coat from the server. He held it out so she could slip into it. Audrey waited for Edward to do the same, but he let the server take care of it. Edward tipped the server generously, making sure that Emma saw the large amount of cash he gave away.

"Well, Emma, I'll see you tomorrow after church," Michael said, grasping the ring box in his pocket.

"Don't keep me waiting, dear," Emma said.

Michael sensed that she knew a proposal was coming. He didn't mind, though.

The group walked through the enchanting bar room and emerged onto the darkened street. Michael extended an umbrella and handed it to Emma, who took the gesture graciously.

"Are you boys headed back to your hotel?" Emma asked.

"Yes, ma'am," Michael said.

Edward tried to hide his smirk.

"It was a pleasure seeing you this evening, Emma," Edward said. "I hope to see much more of you."

Emma nodded toward Edward, and then she grasped Michael's hand gently. She kissed him on the cheek, sending a wave of excitement through his body.

"I love you, dear," Michael said.

"And I love you," Emma said. "I can't wait to see you again tomorrow."

Michael tipped his hat toward Audrey, who waited for a gesture from Edward. Emma smiled at Michael. The image of her eyes imprinted itself into Michael's memory. She turned and strolled into the darkness. As the women turned the corner, Edward relaxed his shoulders; an aura of mischief filled the air.

"You know we're not headed back to our hotel, right?" Edward asked.

"Well, I was hoping to get a decent night of sleep," Michael said.

"Not happening, old chap," Edward said. "It's your last night of freedom. We're going out for one more drink. I know a place over on Third Avenue."

Michael dropped his head and rolled his eyes. He smiled and started the stroll toward Third. Edward patted him on the shoulder approvingly. They walked through an alleyway to cut the distance before emerging onto the main sidewalk again. Michael stepped with a slight wobble, a side effect of too many whiskey drinks. Edward seemed to walk straight, serving as a guide. Michael rarely drank alcohol. His tolerance was low, especially for an Irishman.

As they approached the corner, Michael looked down the street toward the Willamette River. He could almost see the Hawthorne Bridge's towers. Or maybe it was just a water container on top of a brick building. He couldn't be sure; it was dark and his sight was filled with liquor.

"Here we are, Sully," Edward said. "Quimby's. The best joint in town."

Michael looked up at the sign. He had always wanted to grab a drink at Quimby's. There was something about it. He wasn't sure what, exactly, but he knew this bar would provide some excitement.

Edward pushed Michael through the door and followed behind him. The room was dimly lit. Booths with tall backs lined the walls, while compact wooden tables packed the center. A long wooden bar stretched across the back wall. The stained-glass skylight produced dark shades of green throughout the room, cut only by the reflection from the mirror behind the bar.

"Let's head up to the bar and grab a drink," Edward said. "We don't need a table."

"But all these tables are open," Michael said. "There's hardly anyone in here this late."

Edward ignored the request and moved directly to the bar, nodding directly to the bartender.

"Two whiskey glasses, please," Edward said.

The bartender nodded. Edward handed the bartender some cash for the drinks, along with a note he had pulled from his pocket. The bartender poured whiskey quickly into two glasses, but left briefly with the note and returned empty-handed. Michael missed the entire exchange.

"Eddy," Michael said, "I want to thank you so much for tonight. I really needed to cut loose and have a good time. You're a great friend."

Edward shifted nervously from one foot to the other. A bead of sweat formed on his brow, but he wiped it with the back of his hand as he pretended to adjust his fedora.

"I know I keep myself straight out there in the forest,"

Michael continued, "but a night like this really puts things into perspective for me. I need to live a little more. And it all starts tomorrow when I propose to Emma."

Michael raised his whiskey glass and nodded at Edward in appreciation. Edward raised his glass as well, but his face remained stoic.

"I'm sure this will be a night you'll never forget," Edward said.

Edward watched as Michael threw his head back and downed his whiskey. Edward placed his glass on the bar top without touching a drop of his own drink.

"I'm going to head to the restroom," Edward said.

He shifted away from the bar and maneuvered through the wooden tables. As he reached the door to the restroom, he turned and looked at Michael, who stood by the bar admiring the stained-glass skylight. Edward walked through the narrow hallway. Passing the restroom, he exited Quimby's. Rain fell on his hat as he scampered down the sidewalk.

Michael didn't notice. His attention remained fixed on the colors of the skylight. The moonlight beautifully illuminated the stained-glass window.

Click. Snap.

The floorboards under Michael disappeared. Gravity carried him unwillingly through the trapdoor.

He landed hard on the packed dirt beneath Quimby's. Looking up with confusion, he saw only darkness where the trapdoor had snapped open just moments ago.

As he sat stunned on the floor, he looked around for any clues as to where he was, but he only saw darkness, aside from the few light bulbs that hung from the underside of the floorboards above his head.

Michael wanted to stand, but the fall and whiskey kept him seated. Or maybe it was fear.

He heard a grunt and the shuffling of feet. The sound came closer.

"Good night," a voice said in the dark.

The wooden bat smacked Michael in the back of the head.

Blackness.

Chapter 4

Michael's head throbbed. *Damn whiskey*, he thought. He struggled to open his eyes. As he sat upright, his vision began to focus, but his surroundings remained dark, making it difficult to decipher exactly where he was. He knew he wasn't in his own bed. In fact, he didn't think he was in a bed at all.

He moved his arm to rub the back of his head, but something trapped his arms in place; he was shackled to a pole with metal chains.

Michael clawed at the dirt underneath him as panic began to set in. He shook his wrists slowly at first. Then, he jolted them violently. The clanging of the metal shackles grew more real, more constricting. He was trapped.

"Where am I?" Michael muttered. "What's going on?"

He sensed another person rustling near him somewhere in the shadows. Michael curled up, subconsciously protecting himself against hidden danger.

"No sense in worrying too much," a man's voice said. "The three of us don't know where we are either."

Michael squinted his eyes, attempting to see who spoke. His eyes began to adjust to the darkness. A flickering torchlight from the wall helped Michael distinguish a man's face about six feet away. The man was sitting against another pole, likely chained to it. He saw two more figures on nearby poles. Their white eyes illuminated behind their beards from the torch's flame.

"Where are we?" Michael whispered. His hoarse voice masked his shaky conviction.

An eerie laugh echoed from somewhere in the dark.

"I don't know for sure," the man said. "I woke up here a few hours ago. But I would guess we're in the Shanghai Tunnels."

Michael shook his head in bewilderment.

"The Shanghai Tunnels?" Michael asked.

"Never heard of 'em?" another man's voice said from the dark.

"Certainly not," Michael said.

The man laughed quietly. A silhouette of wild hair appeared with the flicker of the torch.

"Well, that means you must not be well-acquainted with the Portland underworld," the man said. "The Shanghai Tunnels are as old as the city itself. They run all through town, except no one sees them. They run underneath every building on this side of the river. At first, they connected the river's shipping docks with business storage facilities. You see, that way, dock workers could run their products straight from the dock to a business on Third Avenue without having to worry about running it through the streets."

Michael raised an eyebrow. He moved his hand to wave off the man's notions, but the shackles stopped his motion before it started.

"Then why are we here?" Michael asked.

The man laughed again.

"You see, once the retaining walls were built along the

Willamette River, people forgot about the tunnels," the man said. "The tunnels were ripe for the taking. Criminals, people who didn't want to be seen, you see. They flocked to the tunnels. Used them for whatever illicit purpose they wanted. No one owns them. No one regulates them. At least not officially."

A strange scent wafted into Michael's nose. He recoiled at the smell, gasping audibly.

"You don't like the smell of opium, boy?" the man said. "That's just one of the many uses of the Shanghai Tunnels. You'll see plenty of women down here too, if we ever get to move away from these shackles."

"Does the opium come from Shanghai?" Michael asked.

"Some of it does, I'm sure," the man said. "But that's not where the name comes from. You see, it's not about what comes in. It's about what goes out."

Michael shivered at the thought. Panic started to set in again. He tried to stand, twisting his body to move the shackles up the pole he was attached to. He took a step to the side and felt a sharp pain dig into his bare feet. His scream echoed through the tunnels.

Collapsing on the dirt, he rubbed his foot with his shackled hand. Hot blood ran down his feet. He felt a large shard of glass embedded in his heel; he pulled it out slowly, releasing another slow-building scream.

"They took your shoes, boy," the man said. "They always do. They took ours too."

Michael scanned the floor around him. As the torchlight flickered, he could make out colorful shards of glass scattered across the floor around them. *They don't want us to escape*, he thought.

Defeated, his body sunk into the dirt. His stomach churned. He wanted to vomit. He wanted to cry, to scream for help, but he knew it would be futile. He cried anyway. He was deep underneath the city. No one could hear his sobs.

Maybe he had fallen asleep. Maybe he passed out. Maybe he was paralyzed with fear and defeat. By the time he heard the footsteps, he wasn't sure how much time had passed. Maybe days, or maybe minutes.

The muffled footsteps moved slowly through the tunnels, stomping on the dirt floor with confidence and authority. Michael turned to see a torchlight approach through a corridor. As it moved closer, the tunnels began to illuminate. Michael sat up, prepared to face whoever carried the torch.

And then he saw him. The man carrying the torch was short and strong. The V-shaped scar on his face repulsed Michael, and his natural scowl implied ferocity. The man moved slowly, but efficiently; dirt and glass crunched under his thick boots. He approached the four men chained to poles. Michael could see that he had been chained into an outcropping, dug into the dirt wall of a tunnel offshoot.

"Stand up," the man said gruffly.

The four men stood without hesitation. The man moved toward the wild-haired storyteller and unlocked one shackle. Looping it around the pole, he reconnected the man's shackle to his wrist. The storyteller was free from the pole, but his arms and legs were still chained together.

"Don't move," the man said.

The storyteller remained still. With the introduction of more torchlight, Michael could see the storyteller's face. He looked old, weathered from years of hard labor. Or maybe it was something else that had decayed him.

Convinced that the storyteller would remain still, the man moved toward Michael. He unshackled Michael's left wrist, unwrapped the chain from the pole, and reattached the shackle to Michael's wrist.

"Don't move," he said to Michael.

Michael nodded. Compliance through fear.

The man moved toward the third prisoner and unshackled him.

"Don't move," the man said to the prisoner.

The man turned to the final prisoner, but the third prisoner moved. Fast. He dashed toward an opening in the tunnels, intent on escape. The guard didn't move; he simply stood and watched as the prisoner ran.

The third prisoner took quick, long steps before disappearing from the torchlight. And then Michael heard a bloodcurdling scream, followed by a solid thud. And then silence.

Smirking, the guard walked slowly toward the third prisoner. He leaned down and picked up the prisoner by the hair. Tugging his body away from the glass shards, the guard pushed the prisoner back to the group. His face gushed with blood. His tattered clothes were sliced and red.

"Do as I say," the guard said.

The guard linked the four men together by their wrist shackles. Michael was in the front of the line.

"Follow me," the guard told Michael. "Do not deviate from my path."

The guard nodded to his left and swung his torch toward the floor, revealing multicolored glass shards everywhere. Terror filled Michael's nerves. His legs shook with fear.

Michael followed the guard closely through the tunnels. He

weaved left and right, making sure the bare-footed prisoners avoided glass.

Musk emerged from the damp earth beneath Michael's feet, marinating from weeks of slow, seeping rain above ground. Ghostly shadows from slivers of torchlight cut through the thick layer of darkness that enveloped Michael's sight. Fear chilled the air, but humidity built from the stale air, palpable to the tongue. The clanking of chains reverberated off the muffled earth walls, while cackles and haunting groans echoed from somewhere distant.

A steady aura of light appeared around a corner. Michael and the three prisoners moved slowly toward it. As they rounded the corner, a room opened up, carved into an alcove in the tunnel's dirt. Bunk beds lined the back wall of the room. Men and women were sitting upright in their individual bunks, smoking opium pipes. A few bunks contained passed out patrons, while others were filled with hysterical laughter.

"There's your opium den, boy," the storyteller whispered to Michael.

The man laughed.

"I've spent some time in this very den," the storyteller continued. "In fact, the last thing I remember is passing out in one of those bunks."

Michael paused. The sight of the opium den enthralled him; the poor people who had resorted to this underground environment mystified him.

"Top bunks are cheaper," the storyteller said. "But it comes with a risk. You don't want an eight-foot fall to ruin your high."

"Keep quiet and keep it moving," the guard said.

With a quick shuffle, Michael continued his walk. The tunnels were dark. The smell of raw earth exuded from the floor, paired with the scent of old wood from the overhead floorboards. Barrels of liquor lined the tunnel walls. Occasionally, a door would appear along the dirt wall, likely leading to the back room of a restaurant or business that needed access to the tunnels.

As the prisoners weaved through the damp maze of subterranean dirt, a red door appeared on the left side of the tunnel. A man moved suspiciously toward it. He knocked twice, paused, and knocked once more. The door opened. A scantily-clad woman opened it, smiled, and pulled him in.

"Ah, another den of sin," the storyteller whispered. "These tunnels are full of underground brothels. I spent some time in a few of them myself."

Michael raised an eyebrow, trying to hide his shock, even though no one could see his face.

As they turned another corner, more light appeared. But this time, it wasn't torch light. Fresh night air filled Michael's lungs. Moonlight flickered off of the Willamette River. An ocean-going vessel was docked against the shore. The captain of the ship stood on the shore, waiting for the guard to bring the prisoners to him.

"Four healthy sailors," the captain said.

He looked at Michael with approval. Then, he noticed the third prisoner's bloody face and shredded clothes.

"Well, three and a half, anyway," he continued.

"Ah, he's fine," the guard said.

The captain held out a stack of cash, which the guard took quickly. He stuffed the cash into his jacket pocket. His V-shaped scar contrasted with his devious smile.

"They're all yours," the guard said.

The captain nodded.

34

"Move it," the captain said to the prisoners.

Michael wanted to fight, to protest, to act courageously. But he couldn't. The sense of defeat and the power of despair clutched him, keeping him fearful, motionless. The captain motioned his head aggressively toward the ship's ramp. Michael led the three prisoners along the ramp up to the ship. Two tall steam towers emerged from the ship, making Michael appear smaller than he already felt. The ramp forced Michael onto a steel deck, where a sailor pushed him toward a door. Michael moved through another tunnel; this one was metal. He navigated through the compact corridors until the sailor pushed the prisoners into a small, empty room. No bunks. No chairs. No windows.

The sailor unshackled each prisoner before turning around and shutting the door. Michael heard the shackles clank against the metal floor as he sat in total darkness.

Chapter 5

Michael jolted awake, but he couldn't see anything. The windowless room removed any trace of light. The smell of salt water and human waste filled the musty steel room. Another person moved against the metal wall near Michael, but he couldn't see who it was. He had no idea how long he had been asleep.

"Hello?" Michael said quietly.

A body moved again somewhere in the dark.

"Hello, there," one of the prisoners replied. "Did you enjoy your rest?"

His raspy voice echoed off the steel walls. Michael laughed at the notion of enjoyment.

"Something like that," Michael said. "Any idea what time it is?"

"No," the man said. "I haven't been awake long."

Michael sat up and leaned against the cold wall. A rivet dug into his back as he forced his weight against it.

"The name's John," the man said.

"Michael."

"Pleasure to make your acquaintance," John said. "What brought you down to the Shanghai Tunnels?"

Michael sat forward and pondered the question. *Eddy?* A

hazy memory appeared in his mind. *Did Eddy give the bartender something at Quimby's?*

"You know, I'm not quite sure," Michael said.

John laughed. It echoed through the holding cell.

"Everyone's got a reason," John said. "I sure do."

Michael remained silent and waited for John to volunteer his story.

"I work for a syndicate in Seattle, you see," John said. "I messed up a little, and I owed some guys a favor, so I came down to Portland to do a job. They sent me to this bar to talk to a guy named Theo. I go up to the bartender and ask for Theo. Next thing I know, I'm being dragged through the kitchen and down some dark staircase and they chain me to a damn pole."

"How little was this mistake you made?" Michael asked.

John laughed. Uncertain about its sincerity, Michael returned the laugh nervously.

Footsteps clanked from somewhere outside the cell. The bolt in the door unlatched; metal grinded on metal. The door creaked open, illuminating the entire metal prison. Michael covered his face to hide his unadjusted eyes from the light.

As his eyes refocused, he looked at the door again. A guard entered the cell and began shouting at the prisoners in a language Michael didn't understand. Michael slowly stood to his feet, following the guard's upward hand signals.

Looking around the cell, Michael could finally see the other prisoners. John was short and round. His bald head and beard stubble projected a gruff exterior. As Michael scanned his eyes to the next prisoner, he shuddered at the gashes and caked blood on the man's face. *Where's the fourth guy?*

The prison guard marched to the back of the cell. Near a shadowy corner, he knelt down, inspecting something.

Shouting in a language that Michael didn't understand, he motioned for another guard to join him. Together, the guards pulled the fourth prisoner into the light. The storyteller, an old man with chaotic gray hair, lay dead on the ground. His face had lost any sense of coloring that indicated life. The guards checked his pulse after slapping him in the face, just to make sure he was actually dead.

"Why do they keep bringing in these guys from opium dens?" a guard said.

The other guard shrugged his shoulders and responded in a foreign language. He motioned for the three prisoners to follow him out of the cell. Michael's bare feet felt cold on the steel floor. His blue suit pants were filthy from the dirt. His white shirt was tattered and scuffed. His vest had lost a button. And he had lost his hat.

Rubbing his hand on his wrist, he noticed that his wrists were no longer shackled. As he took a long step out of the cell and into the ship's corridor, he realized that his feet weren't shackled either. Now he could make a run for it.

One guard walked in front of the prisoners, while the other guard followed the line. Michael wasn't sure where they were going, but he knew that he would run as soon as the guards gave him an opportunity.

The narrow corridor led to a staircase. Grooved metal dug into Michael's feet, which were accustomed to protective boots. The guard opened a door at the top of the staircase, letting in intolerable sunlight and chilled, salty air. Michael passed through the doorway and entered the deck of the ship.

Ocean. Endless ocean. Everywhere.

Michael moved toward the ship's railing and peered into the horizon. All he saw was churning, violent water in every direction. Any possibility of escape had vanished.

"Stand in line," one of the guards shouted.

Michael joined John and the third prisoner in a shabby line in front of the guard near the middle of the deck. The guard stood before them silently. An older man with a captain's hat stepped down a short set of stairs. He approached the prisoners slowly, methodically. The guard nodded and left the group, returning into the depths of the ship from where he came.

"Welcome to the Pacific Ocean, gentlemen," the captain said.

He looked around at the view, admiring the vast, formless landscape. The smirk on his face sent an eerie chill into the pit of Michael's nerves.

"We're a few hundred miles away from Portland at this point," the captain continued. "And if everything goes according to plan, we won't see another ship until we reach Shanghai."

"Shanghai?" the third prisoner said. "As in *China*?"

"Yes, boy," the captain said.

The prisoner looked at Michael and John for support. Michael's fear of the captain's smirk forced him to remain emotionless.

"Why in the hell are we headed to Shanghai?" the prisoner asked.

The captain's laughter boomed throughout the deck. Crew members joined in, laughing at the prisoners in a chorus of horror. Some pointed, hyperbolizing their side-splitting laughter.

"You three must have pissed someone off pretty badly," the captain said. "You see, gentlemen, someone sold you to me as slaves."

Michael's stomach turned. And it turned again. He wanted to throw up. He knelt down, sinking his knee into a puddle of salt water.

"Stand up, boy," the captain shouted.

Michael staggered upward. John held out an arm; Michael grabbed onto it, stabilizing himself as he caught his breath.

"You'll work for me while you're on the ship, of course," the captain said. "And once we get to Shanghai, I'll take you to the market and sell you to the highest bidder. I'll make a profit from the price I bought you for, naturally. I always make a point to sell my merchandise to families that treat their servants well, but I can't make any promises."

The captain turned to a crew member and laughed again. His dark beard shook; his tattooed forearms projected outward. The booming laughter made Michael shiver.

The third prisoner's hand twitched. He rubbed his face vigorously, pressing his palms against the gashes in his cheek. The captain eyed him strangely.

And then he did it. The third prisoner turned quickly. He sprinted toward the railing. Planting his feet, the prisoner jumped onto the railing, climbing it with ferocity. He turned to look at the ship; a shred of doubt crossed his face. A guard pulled his gun and shot at the prisoner; the bullet ricocheted off the cross beam. Adrenaline kicked in. The prisoner sprung off the railing and fell feet-first toward the sea. Michael didn't hear a splash over the roaring ocean.

"The sea will take him," the captain said. "Not my concern. That just increased your value, gentlemen. I wouldn't advise following in your friend's footsteps, though. No one knows where you are. We cover our tracks to precision. No one will ever know where or how to find you. You'll likely be pronounced dead. As far as you're concerned, you no longer exist."

The captain laughed again before turning and leaving the prisoners in charge of the second guard.

"Supply and demand, gentlemen," the captain shouted. "Supply and demand."

The guard shouted at the prisoners in Chinese. His force and hand gestures told Michael to return to the cell. The door closed tightly behind him as he returned down the dark, steel hallway. Trapped.

Chapter 6

The cold wind blew salt water onto the ship's deck. Sun beat down on Michael's back as he knelt down to scrub the salt off the floor. The combination of intense direct sunlight and chilled wind confused his senses. Licking his dry lips, he couldn't decipher his sweat from sea water. He needed a drink badly.

Water, water everywhere and not a drop to drink, he thought. *Whoever created that mantra must have been in my position.*

Michael wasn't sure how long he had been at sea, or how far he had travelled from Portland. Maybe it had been days. Maybe weeks. Perhaps a few months. He had lost count of the nightly storms and the chilling wind, the beatings and sea sickness, the solitude and the agony.

He wondered if this was some sort of long nightmare. But it felt real enough.

Every day brought the same routine. First, Michael woke up in the dark, windowless cell. He smelled urine and rust; he shivered from the cold steel that served as his mattress. The door creaked open and a guard tossed two plates of alleged food onto the floor, along with two cups of water. Michael choked down his food while John did the same. The guards told the two prisoners to rise and march to the deck, where they received orders from the second mate, who gave them the jobs that even the lowliest sailor wouldn't dare accomplish. Michael and John cleaned toilets, scrubbed the sides of the ship while hanging from ropes, cleaned the crew's clothes, and climbed high above the ship to repair minor inflictions. The captain didn't mind; as long as these two didn't die on the journey, he would make a profit.

Michael felt comfortable working hard in the forest. But that was by his own choosing, and this wasn't the forest. He hadn't found his sea legs yet, which meant he vomited over the ship's railing almost every day. The captain forced John and Michael to complete their duties in stormy weather, even when he called the regular crew inside for safety. Waves crashed onto the ship's deck, sending rushing water across Michael's path.

If Michael refused to complete a task, he was beaten. Sometimes he was starved. Sometimes he was publicly ridiculed by the crew members on the ship, who he had started to regard as pirates. He had grown numb to it to some extent.

When the crew went in for dinner each night, Michael and John had to stay on the deck, performing their tasks until the sun set, which wasn't much of a relief. Sunset meant the guards forced Michael and John back into their windowless cell to scarf down another meager meal, just enough food to help them recognize their own hunger, just enough food to help them remember what they were missing.

Days like this, sunny and breezy, used to give Michael a reason for joy. But the heat and corrosive salt water eroded Michael's composure, like rust on shackles.

John scrubbed the deck in silence next to Michael. He chewed his lip in frustration, a rage that he channeled toward every rust stain on the deck.

"I'm done with this, mate," John said.

Michael looked over at John, who sat down cross-legged on the floor, setting his sponge beside him. John wiped his forehead with his sleeve. A guard strolled around the corner and inspected the work of the cleaning crew.

"Johnny," Michael whispered, "guard's coming. Start scrubbing."

John turned and looked at the guard. He returned his attention to Michael.

"Don't want to," John said. "I'm over it."

The guard noticed John sitting and relaxing. His steps quickened as he made a straight path toward John.

"Get back to work!" the guard shouted.

"No," John said.

The guard's eyebrow raised. Michael avoided eye contact; he didn't want to get in trouble too. His back had finally recovered from his own attempt at work avoidance.

From his hip belt, the guard removed a club. It glinted in the harsh sunlight. He held the club in front of John's face, hoping that the sight of it would force John to work.

It didn't.

The guard reached the club back and swung it forward with power. The club landed directly on John's shoulder, sending him wrenching to the floor. John curled into a ball and prepared for the next blow. John writhed with pain from the club's violence. The guard swung a third time and cracked John in the back.

As the guard pulled the club back for a fourth swing, Michael stood and grabbed the guard's arm. Throwing the guard to the floor, Michael watched the club fall to his feet. He reached for it, grabbing it by the handle. Power pulsed through his arm. He swung the club above him; the guard's head was in his sights. But before he cracked the club onto the guard's skull, he paused. Seeing John wrestle with pain gave Michael a feeling of regret; he didn't want to inflict that kind of pain on anyone, not even the guard who had mistreated him day after day.

Michael dropped the club. Another guard sprinted toward him, tackling him to the ground. With the guard's elbow in his back, the other guard kicked Michael in the ribs. His breath left him.

The storm started just before sunset. Rain drove down from the black clouds. Waves crashed into the sides of the ship; a familiar knot began to form in Michael's stomach. His bruised ribs made it feel worse.

The guards appeared and shouted at John and Michael in Chinese to return to their cell quickly. The prisoners complied; their resistance efforts had been depleted.

Stepping into the dark, windowless cell, Michael sat on the floor in his customary corner. The guards dropped two plates of food and two cups of water on the floor. Michael scarfed his food to calm his nausea.

After his eyes adjusted to the dark, Michael went to work removing a loose bolt in the wall. He had been working on it for the last few nights; he hoped that it would provide a little light for their cell. And when the bolt came free, a stream of light entered the room, giving him just enough light to play cards.

"We can finally use these," John said. "I still can't believe I was able to snatch these from that cook's jacket without getting caught. I guess my old skills are still useful."

Michael laughed; it was the first time he had laughed in a while. John dealt five cards to Michael, and five to himself.

"The name of the game is poker," John said. "We don't have much to bet with, but at least it's something to do."

Michael nodded in agreement. Anything to take his mind off of the agony of isolation.

He picked up his cards and fanned them out; he saw a five, a seven, a queen, and two aces. He placed the five and seven on the ground and John dealt him two more cards: a queen and a two. For the final round, Michael returned the two and received a new card: another queen. He tried to hide the smile that began to surface.

"Alright, Mikey," John said. "What do you have?"

Michael displayed his cards on the ground for John to see.

"Full house," Michael said.

John tossed his cards into a pile in front of him.

"And I thought I had you beat with my three jacks," John said.

Michael grabbed the deck of cards, shuffled, and dealt another round. They played for a while in silence, interrupted occasionally by clanking footsteps down the hallway and creaking metal from the ship's hull.

"I was talking with a crew member today," John said.

Michael looked up from his poor hand and raised an eyebrow, which encouraged John to keep talking.

"I asked him what it was going to be like when we got to Shanghai," John continued. "If we think this ship is bad, Shanghai will be worse."

Michael put his cards down on the floor.

"What do you mean?" Michael asked.

"The guy told me this," John said. "We'll arrive at the port in Shanghai and be carted off with our hands tied up. No chance of running away. They'll pull us through some back alleys where we can't flag down anyone for help. Then, at night, they'll pull us into some back room and force us in front of a small crowd. People will bid on us to be their slaves while the captain pokes at us and shows us off, like we're some prize cattle."

Michael picked his cards back up again. He placed three cards on the ground and exchanged them for three more.

"At least we can get to work in some farmhouse," Michael said. "It can't be as bad as this ship."

"That's the thing," John said. "It'll be worse. The crewman told me that these people who buy American slaves are terrible. Mostly American and British folks trying to run illicit operations out of Chinese ports. The Chinese government doesn't want them there, but it's hard to argue with a machine gun. These guys run shady operations in factories that produce opium and stuff like that. They won't feed us hardly at all. They'll beat us every day just for fun; more if we don't work fast enough. We might not ever see the sun again. We might not even survive five years in those conditions."

Michael set his cards down again; he had lost his interest in poker.

"We have to get out of here," John continued.

John could see Michael's despair as he retreated to his usual corner. The stream of light reflected off of Michael's silent tears.

"We'll figure something out," John said. "We have to."

He moved to his own corner of the cell. The sound of card shuffling echoed off the steel walls.

Michael curled up on the floor, shivering from the cold. He tucked his chin underneath his collar. He thought about home, about Portland. His thoughts drifted to Emma. She was probably continuing a frantic search for Michael through the city.

His thoughts froze as they floated into murky waters.

Maybe she had forgotten about Michael. Or worse. Maybe she didn't care that he was gone.

He hoped someone was looking out for Emma, helping her find Michael. Perhaps Edward had taken up the task.

He thought about what Edward was doing. He had probably returned to the forest, to logging. But logging was only temporary for Edward. He always had grand plans to become something bigger, to regain his footing in society. Edward was the last face Michael remembered before he fell.

It couldn't have been Eddy, Michael thought. *He wouldn't have done this to me.*

The thought simmered in his mind. He tried to replay the night at Quimby's in his memories, but the memories were too blurry, too infused with whiskey.

But the thought still lingered. Edward was there. He led Michael to Quimby's specifically. And he had been talking about a plan to regain his wealth. Maybe Michael's disappearance played into Edward's plan.

Michael seethed in anger. He wanted to shout, to smash the steel walls that caged him.

Soon, that anger turned to a helplessness that morphed quickly into despair.

The floor seemed to grow colder, forcing Michael to shiver. As Michael shifted his weight toward the wall, his hand caught some rope fibers that came loose. They were probably remnants of the countless rope cuffs the guards used on prisoners that had occupied the cell. Michael sat up; he braided the rope strands methodically as he pondered possibilities for escape.

John snored in the corner of the cell. Michael remained alert, braiding together every inch of rope he could find. Eventually, he had enough rope to make a decent necklace. Reaching into his pocket, he removed the small box that held Emma's wedding ring. He removed the ring, tossed the box in the corner of the cell, and looped the ring through the rope. He tied the ends of the rope together and placed the necklace over his head. Emma's ring dangled near his heart.

I'll find a way to return to you, my love, Michael thought. *I must*.

Chapter 7

Michael jolted awake. The ship lurched again, sending John rolling across the floor. Michael reached toward his heart and felt Emma's ring, which provided a sense of calm strength. The smell of salty air had lessened overnight.

Footsteps echoed down the hallway, followed by the familiar creak of the door bolt. But something was different. As the door opened, little light illuminated the cell. The guard didn't throw food on the ground as he usually did each morning either. In fact, this guard seemed unfamiliar.

"We've arrived in Shanghai early," the guard said. "It's still too late at night for us to remove you from the ship, but inspectors will be moving through our ship to look at our cargo. If you make a sound while they're here, I'll kill you myself. At first light, we'll remove you from the ship with the rest of our legitimate cargo. Do you understand?"

Both prisoners nodded groggily.

"Good," the guard said. "Now go back to sleep and don't make a sound."

The guard turned and slammed the steel door, extinguishing all light, except the small sliver that entered through the bolt hole. Michael laid down in his corner; sleep still filled his eyes.

His consciousness began to drift, but then he jolted upright. Adrenaline coursed through his body.

"John," Michael said. "Did you hear that?"

"Hear what?" John said.

"The guard closed the door," Michael said. "But I didn't hear him latch the bolt."

John sat up abruptly in his corner. He stepped to John's side of the cell and grabbed him by the shoulder.

"This is our chance," John said. "We won't have another one."

Michael nodded in agreement. He peered through the bolt hole in the steel wall, which gave him an obstructed view of the hallway. A guard sprinted through the corridor and Michael heard his footsteps clink up the metal-grated stairs. He motioned toward the door.

With silent precision, John pushed the door open. He scanned the hallway as his head emerged from the darkness. Not a guard in sight. Motioning to Michael, the prisoners left the cell and sprinted down the corridor, their bare feet silent on the cold metal floor.

The familiar staircase rose in front of them; the prisoners sprinted toward the door at the top, but they stopped short. The door opened, sending John and Michael scurrying into the shadows behind the stairs. A guard dashed down the steps; his foot was so close that Michael could smell the salt water on the guard's shoe in front of his face. The guard sprinted down the hallway and blew by the prisoner cell; his focus was elsewhere.

As the guard disappeared into another corridor, the prisoners scampered out from behind the staircase and climbed it. Michael opened the door slowly, checking the deck before fully emerging. Sliding behind some stacked cargo boxes, the prisoners waited in the shadows.

The ship's deck was dark, lit only by a half moon. *It must be midnight*, Michael thought. The smell of rusty saltwater hung in the air, but he sensed something new. Humidity. The air was thick. Fragrant jungle wafted across the port. He couldn't see it through the blackness, but he knew it was there.

Michael peered from behind the boxes. He saw half-lit shadows move purposefully across the deck. The pirate crew prepared to be boarded by a customs agent. They aimed to cover any clues about their illicit cargo.

The dock was illuminated slightly by torchlight. Michael could barely see it in the distance. They could make it if they jumped, but they would have to swim.

Michael shifted back behind the boxes; the captain's voice boomed across the deck.

"Get those opium boxes buried beneath the wheat supply," the captain shouted. "The customs boat will be here any minute. And hide those Portland slaves in the smuggling compartments beneath the corridor floor. Go get them now!"

Michael's heart raced faster. Once the crew discovered his absence, they would start a manhunt. He looked at John, who already knew the plan.

Moving away from the safety of the cargo boxes, the prisoners scurried across the deck, pausing briefly to hide behind large pipes and the occasional wall.

With the edge of the ship in sight, Michael heard the captain's voice boom louder.

"What?" he shouted. "Which one of you idiots left the cell door unlocked?"

Panic scattered across the ship's deck. Light from torches and flashlights scanned the main level, sending Michael and

John ducking behind a barrel near the edge of the ship. Michael's heart raced faster. His breath quickened. He felt like passing out.

"Come on, Mikey," John said. "It has to be now."

Fear gripped Michael as he tightened his leg muscles, preparing to sprint. But he froze. A guard's flashlight placed the prisoners in full view. Michael couldn't see the guard. He was obscured by the light, but the cruel laughter made the guard's presence known.

"I got 'em!" the guard shouted.

A shadowy figure appeared next to the guard; his face flickered under torchlight. The familiar prison guard glared intently at Michael and Johnny. His face pulsed with cold determination.

"Round 'em up," the other guard said.

As the flashlight moved forward, Michael sprinted across the deck. John followed, just one step behind him. As the prisoners dashed through open space, flashlights attempted to keep them in sight. Gunshots ricocheted off the ship's steel, sending Michael darting across the deck to avoid the bullets. Instinct and fear overtook any sense of caution and rationality.

The railing was approaching fast. Michael knew he had one choice: jump.

He took one final dash before he dug his feet into the deck, springing forward with all the strength he could muster. As the railing passed beneath his feet, Michael felt the sensation of freefall. His stomach lifted. His breath quickened. Nerves fired up his spine, sending reflexes to his brain. He swung his arms subconsciously, trying to fly his way back to the ship.

Time slowed.

He hung in the air.

He couldn't see anything on the shore in front of him, just a few lights in the distance.

And then his feet slapped the water. He sunk into the dark ocean. He lost all sense of direction. Panic began to overtake his nerves, causing him to flail against the current. He kicked and kicked, hoping he was moving in the right direction, holding back his need to gasp for air.

Then, his hands broke through the underwater prison, emerging into freedom. The salty air sent fire through Michael's lungs.

He bounced above the water's surface and scanned through the darkness.

John splashed into the ocean next to him. As Michael watched John emerge from the ocean, he recoiled. Gunshots fired from the ship's deck into the darkness, hoping to get lucky. Michael swam as fast as his tired body would let him. The absence of shoes allowed him to swim faster. Bullets sunk into the ocean around Michael, fueling his adrenaline.

"Where'd they go?" the captain shouted from the deck.

Michael could see a torchlight in the distance; it barely illuminated the dock. He found an old ladder attached the side of a wooden platform and climbed it, stopping at the top to see if any guards waited to capture him. Seeing the dock empty, Michael and John sprinted down the rows of wood planks. Their bare feet muffled any trace of sound, but the old wood dug splinters into their soles.

As they reached the end of the dock, they turned onto a dirt road lined with dense vegetation and continued their run. Water evaporated and turned to sweat on Michael's shirt. His lungs gasped for air. The road seemed never-ending in the darkness, but a faint glow beckoned Michael to keep running.

The road curved along with the ocean before turning into a small bay. Michael's legs began to scream, but he knew that, if he stopped, he was dead. He needed to hold out a little longer.

And that's when he saw it.

The lights. The people. The hustle.

They were in Shanghai.

Chapter 8

About once each week, the *Portland Daily* made its way into the Oregon wilderness. Michael clamored for it, wanting to read the latest updates in world politics and city drama. He considered himself decently aware of global news, but he didn't know much about China.

He did know that China had gone through a revolution a few years ago. The people overthrew the dynastic system that had existed for thousands of years. The Opium Wars against Great Britain hadn't gone well for China. Now, the country was in the midst of figuring out how to operate its new republic.

Sun Yat-sen controlled the republic, but China was by no means unified. He knew there were certain places in the country that operated under the control of warlords, anxious to grab power in the absence of imperial authority.

He also knew that western powers, like the United States and Great Britain, were starting to gain footholds on China's coastline. Great Britain acquired some pirate port called Hong Kong not long ago. And the United States was inching its way into China too.

The city that swirled in the center of this conflict was Shanghai. Sun Yat-Sen didn't have complete control over the city. Western powers used the city as an entry point into trade with China. And warlords handled the day-to-day operations.

Shanghai was a wild outpost. A den of trouble. One Shanghai resident went so far as to call it a "city of devils."

* * *

As Michael and John sprinted through alleyways and side roads, they understood the implications of Shanghai. Prostitutes stood on corners beckoning weary sailors into their brothels. Gambling houses operated in the open. Opium dens filled back alley tenements. And saloons coaxed thirsty visitors to tempt their own fate.

As the sun began to rise over the city, Michael ducked into an alleyway. John followed. Michael's lungs begged for air. He barged through the first door he saw, sending him sprawling into a bar. The room was empty, aside from the bartender who stood behind the bar polishing cups.

"A little early for a drink," the bartender said. His British accent seemed to fit in well with the Chinese city, oddly enough.

Michael gasped for enough air to speak.

"We're not here for liquor," Michael said.

The bartender smiled, set his glass on the counter, and leaned against the bar.

"Welcome to Blood Alley, boys," the bartender said. "If you're not here for a drink, what other vice can I guide you toward?"

Michael looked at John, who sat down in a wooden chair with his head on the table. His level of fitness didn't match Michael's, who used to spend most of his time chopping down trees.

"We need a place to hide," Michael said.

The bartender smirked. He double-checked that the bar was empty, and then motioned for the prisoners to follow him into the back office. Michael looked at John for reassurance; in return, he received nothing but a panicked, haggard stare. Dimly lit, Michael could hardly see as he followed the bartender through the maze of shadowy, wooden hallways. Uneven floorboards felt rough under Michael's bare feet. The stench of old beer and general filth wafted into his nostrils, slightly reminiscent of the Shanghai Tunnels.

The prisoners moved into a small room with a desk. Papers and liquor bottles covered most of the space, leaving little room for much else. The bartender closed the door and sat in a worn leather chair, which forced Michael and John to stand. They stood confrontationally, yet they sunk from exhaustion.

"So, who are we hiding you from?" the bartender asked.

Michael waited for John to respond. He assumed that John's shady history brought a skillset with it for this type of situation.

But John remained silent. His nerves shook. The courage he projected on the ship had vanished. Or maybe it was never there to begin with. Michael eyed the bartender; he couldn't decide whether or not to trust him. But, since his options were limited, he decided to test the man's ethics.

"We were kidnapped in Portland," Michael began. "I'm not sure who did it, but we ended up on a ship in the middle of the Pacific Ocean. These pirates said they were going to sell us into slavery here in Shanghai."

Leaning back in his chair, the bartender shook his head.

"They Shanghaied you, eh?" he said. "Happens all the time to poor, drunk chaps like you."

Michael's eyes drifted downward, embarrassed for drinking too much at Quimby's. It seemed like years had passed since then.

"I won't ask how you escaped," the bartender continued. "The less I know, the easier it is for me to lie."

John nodded to Michael, approving of the bartender's ethical conviction.

"I can hide you from the ship's crew," the bartender continued. "But you'll have to do something for me, something in return. It'll be dangerous, but it seems to me that you don't have much of a choice."

Shouting echoed through the bar's main room. The voices moved closer to the back room office.

"Bartender!" the voice shouted. "Tell us where you hid 'em!"

The bartender raised an eyebrow at the prisoners; his leverage increased as the voices moved closer. Michael nodded, agreeing to his terms. Standing slowly from his chair, the bartender yelled at the pirates to calm down. He nudged John aside and stepped into the hallway, closing the door behind him to keep the prisoners hidden.

The bartender moved the group of pirates into the bar's main room. Michael put his ear against the wall. The voices were slightly muffled, but he could hear them clearly enough.

"What's he going to have us do?" John whispered.

Michael snapped at John, implying the importance for silence. John pressed his ear against the wall, too.

"Let me pour you chaps a drink," the bartender said.

Five trickles echoed through the wall, indicating five drinks, and five pirates in the bar. After a few seconds of silence, five glasses slammed on the bar top, indicating that all five drinks were quickly consumed.

"We docked at Shanghai Harbor around midnight," one pirate said. "Early this morning, before sunrise, two prisoners escaped. We fear they might be a threat to this community. A suggestive woman down the road told us that she saw two guys run in here about ten minutes ago."

The pirate's inflection suggested that the bartender knew exactly what purpose the prisoners served to the captain.

"I'm not sure you have to worry about the safety of people who stumble into Blood Alley," the bartender said. "And I haven't had anyone come in here this morning except for you gents. It's a little early for the usual bar crowd."

His chuckle boomed through the walls. Silence in the main bar room worried Michael; he wished he could see the pirates' faces.

"If I see anything suspicious," the bartender continued, "I'll send someone down to the docks and let you know."

After what seemed like an endless pause, the pirates stomped through the bar and left. They slammed the door as they exited, sending reverberations into the back room. The bartender waited for a few minutes before returning to his office to check on his fugitives.

"Well, gents," the bartender said, "it looks like you're in the clear for a while."

The bartender stood in the open doorway. His frame filled the entire portal.

"Thank you, sir," Michael said.

"I'm sure you're exhausted," the bartender said. "I'll bring some food and water back here for you. Get some rest. I'll need you ready to work tonight. It's time you fulfilled your end of the bargain."

John stepped forward with conviction.

"Say, bartender," John said. "What kind of work will you have us doing anyway? I'd like to know before I enter into some shady deal."

The bartender's gold tooth glimmered as he smirked.

"You talk like you have another option," the bartender said.

John's confidence deflated. His shoulder sunk and his head dropped.

"It would just be nice to know, is all," John said. "Just tell us what we'll be doing."

"You'll see, gentlemen," the bartender said. "You'll see."

Chapter 9

shouts and crowd noise echoed into the storeroom. Michael slowly opened his eyes, stretching his legs to loosen his knees. Uneven floorboards jabbed into his ribs. The stench of stale beer filled his nostrils. The room was almost as dark as the cell on the ship, but candlelight from the bar drifted in through holes in the wooden wall boards, which provided enough light to see. John snored in the corner of the small room; he was curled up against a small stack of firewood.

"John," Michael whispered. "John, wake up."

Cracking his neck as he rose from the floor, John sat upright and looked groggily at Michael.

"What time is it?" John asked.

Michael looked around for a clock, but found nothing that indicated the time. But, based on the crowd's volume and presumed level of drunkenness, it was late.

"I think we slept through the whole day," Michael said.

"I get the feeling this neighborhood doesn't really get going until after dark," John said.

"Should we make a break for it before we're forced into bartending?" John whispered.

Michael laughed, though the idea had crossed his mind already. The bartender's elusiveness frightened him, but

Michael's ethical code and commitment to his word forced him to stay. *Catholic guilt*, Michael thought.

Quick, thundering footsteps began to distinguish themselves from the rest of the crowd noise. As the footsteps grew louder, Michael's nerves fired. He stood up and prepared for what would come through the door.

The bartender burst through it. He smelled of liquor; his red face glared at the prisoners.

"Wake up, gents. Time to carry out your end of the bargain," he said. His slurred British accent was difficult for Michael to decipher.

"What do you need us to do?" John asked.

"There's a man in the bar who needs you to deliver two packages to another establishment across town," the bartender said.

"What's in the package?" John asked.

"This package contains a large supply of opium, so don't lose it. It's worth a lot of money. Much more money than you're worth."

John stepped forward in protest.

"No," John said. "We're not going to run drugs for you in exchange for a mediocre night of sleep and some stale biscuits."

The bartender stepped forward and crossed his arms, towering above John, whose usual smirk was suddenly absent.

"You're forgetting something gents," the bartender said. "All I have to do is send a message to the docks, and it's slavery for the both of you."

Michael looked at John with sympathy. He didn't want to contribute to this den of vice, but he didn't see another option. His look to John conveyed the situation: they had to do it.

Stepping forward, Michael followed the bartender into the

barroom. John walked behind Michael; he scanned the room looking for any sign of danger. The crowd wasn't as large as its collective voice indicated, but they were raucous. Sailors chugged beer by the pint. Suave thugs and gruff henchmen sipped shots as they eyed the crowd. Scantily-clad women perused through the tables as men in sharp suits played cards. The bartender pointed out a tall man with a white fedora standing at a tall table near the back of the bar. Two suitcases sat in chairs at the table while the man stood by stoically. He nodded at the bartender from across the room, drawing the prisoners to him with a commanding presence.

As Michael and John approached, the man distanced himself slightly and adjusted his attention away from the prisoners. He didn't want to give anyone the impression that he was actually talking to the rough-cut pair.

"You'll take these two suitcases to a man named Herbert," the man said. "He operates the Scorpion Club about a half-mile west."

"Do you have a map?" John asked sarcastically.

The man's eyes flared momentarily before returning to an unusual calm.

"Everyone knows where the Scorpion Club is," the man said. "You'll find it."

Michael looked to the bartender for support, but he seemed to remain still with respect. Or maybe it was fear that kept him locked in place. Michael wondered what type of leverage this man had on the bartender.

As the man reached upward to adjust his fedora, his jacket flapped open slightly. Michael saw the edge of a gun attached to a shoulder holster; Michael's legs began to twitch, an impulse that happened occasionally when he grew anxious.

"How will we know who Herbert is?" John asked.

"He'll find you," the man said. "Take the suitcases and leave. If I hear that you were unable to complete the job, you'll wish you had stayed on that slave ship."

Michael's eyes widened. The implication was clear.

John stepped forward and grabbed one suitcase. He glared up at the man without fear of consequence. Michael snagged the second suitcase and avoided eye contact with the man. The suitcase felt heavy in Michael's hand. Its handle was worn. Michael had the feeling that he wasn't the first one to make a run like this. As the prisoners weaved through the crowd, the bartender's laugh boomed through the noise.

Humidity blasted Michael as he exited the building, but the light breeze cooled him simultaneously. A half-moon hung in the sky, but long clouds covered most of the stars. The dirt road melted under Michael's bare feet. He had almost forgotten what it felt like to wear shoes. The smell of his ragged clothes had become normal. His beard had grown significantly, and his usually well-combed hair flopped around his head.

Moving through the dark alleyway, they emerged onto a slightly larger side street. A woman stood outside of an unmarked door. She watched the prisoners as they wandered aimlessly west. As she stepped forward from the wall, Michael felt defensive.

"You boys looking for anything in particular?" she asked.

"I wish," John said.

The woman cackled eerily. John sauntered toward her, but Michael stuck his arm out to stop him.

"The Scorpion Club," Michael said.

The woman eyed John and shrugged her shoulders before turning her gaze to Michael.

"Turn right," she said. "Follow this street until you reach the river. You'll see the sign."

John nodded with an accompanying smirk. The prisoners walked with enhanced purpose, passing countless bars, casinos, brothels, and night clubs. Cars and horses passed occasionally along the middle of the street, but they ignored the prisoners. Eventually, they saw red neon lights reflect off the river, illuminating the dark road.

"This place looks pretty upscale," John said. "We can't walk in the front door looking like this."

Michael looked at his tattered shirt and bare feet. They were caked in mud and grit.

The prisoners walked into the alley that lined the Scorpion Club. John knocked on the door and a pair of intimidating eyes appeared in the sliding window.

"We're looking for Herbert," John said.

The guard slammed the sliding window. Michael heard bolts crank behind the metal door before it popped open. A large guard waved them in and quickly shut the door behind them. He pointed down the dark hallway and returned to his post.

Loud jazz music echoed through the hallway. As the prisoners walked, they passed an opening that led to the main ballroom. Michael stopped and leaned against the wall. The well-lit room revealed people dressed in expensive suits and short, glamorous dresses, people dancing on the large ballroom floor. Waiters carried wine bottles and cocktails on silver platers. Red leather booths lined the room, and elaborate food platters graced each table.

John tugged on Michael's arm, snapping him from his daze.

"I have a feeling that's not where we're headed," John said.

Michael nodded and followed John down the dark hallway.

As they moved further from the dance hall, the jazz music faded. Their own footsteps echoed off the hallway walls. A room emerged; candlelight flickered from it. A squat man in a pinstripe suit stood to meet them at the door frame.

"We're looking for Herbert," Michael said.

"You've got him," Herbert said. "I've been expecting you."

Herbert motioned for the prisoners to place their suitcases on the table. He opened them both, checked the product, and closed the suitcases. Herbert waved his hand and another man emerged from a darkened hallway to retrieve the suitcases, disappearing again into the depth of the room's darkness.

Michael peered through the flickering candlelight into the shadows. He heard groans and cackles echo through its chambers. The stench of opium smoke drifted in from the caverns.

"The dens are back there," Herbert said. "You see, we provide a service to those seeking refuge from the stresses of daily life. Thank you for helping us provide that service."

John nodded to show his gratitude at the compliment; Michael remained motionless.

A high-pitched wail, followed by low gurgles emitted from the den. Other voices began to whisper hauntingly. A few shouted for help.

"Hey, get back there," Herbert shouted to one of his assistants. "I don't want that man to die in my joint. Grab him and throw him into the next alley."

Michael's eyes widened. One of Herbert's men walked into the opium den, snatched a convulsing man from a top bunk, and dragged him through a dark hallway into another back alley. The man disappeared from view, but Michael could still hear his scream.

Herbert returned his attention calmly to Michael and John. He smiled, wiped his forehead with a cloth, and regained his composure.

"I have a proposition for you," Herbert said. "I would like you both to continue making runs for our organization. Mostly between various bars around town, collecting suitcases and returning them here. Sometimes to the docks."

John smirked and lifted his head with authority.

"We won't do any more runs for free," John said. "We've completed our deal."

"Of course," Herbert said. "You would be well-compensated. We have rooms available above the club that you would stay in."

Herbert scanned their clothes; his face expressed disapproval.

"And we could certainly get you out of these rags," he continued.

Michael shook his head vehemently.

"No," Michael said. "Absolutely not. Thank you for the offer, but I'm out. I can't contribute to this."

John looked at Michael in shock; he thought this sounded like the offer of a lifetime. In fact, John had been employed in an operation much like this in Seattle prior to his capture. It was a fresh start. Michael, however, couldn't succumb to this greed. Herbert smirked and looked at Michael with leverage.

"You do have a choice here, gentlemen," Herbert said. "You can make daily deliveries and live like kings. Or, you can decline my offer. However, if you decline, I can't ignore the fact that you've seen where and how I operate. That's a loose end I can't allow."

Michael's eyes widened with fear. Powerlessness gripped

him. His breath quickened. His nerves fired. His face twitched with anger.

Herbert smiled knowingly. He raised his hand and waved into the dark. An assistant appeared carrying two more suitcases. Placing the suitcases on the table, the assistant opened them, revealing currencies in various colors and numerical values. Locking the suitcases back up, Herbert handed them to Michael and John.

"Deliver these to Le Piege in the French part of town," Herbert said. "In exchange, they'll give you two more suitcases, which you will return promptly to me."

Herbert smirked with a sense of superiority, of presumed authority. Michael grabbed a suitcase and stormed down the dark hallway. Blazing by the well-lit dance hall, he pushed the door open and returned to the night air.

Chapter 10

John jogged to catch up to Michael, who walked briskly down the alleyway. The suitcase swung heavily in his left hand. Red light from the sign illuminated his path.

"Michael," John shouted. "Hold on a minute."

As he stopped and leaned against a brick wall, Michael set his suitcase on the ground and crossed his arms in frustration. His hands shook. He couldn't decide whether they shook from fear, anger, desperation, or some combination of all three.

He thought of Emma. He hoped she was waiting for him patiently somewhere in Portland. He knew he may never see her again. He recognized that he was trapped in Shanghai and may never escape.

Collapsing to his knees in the dirt, he prayed, begging God and Emma to continue the search, hoping that the Portland Police had some clue as to where he was, wishing that they would send a team to rescue him from the clutches of despair.

But his hope soon fluttered away, replaced by silent tears.

He looked down at his suit; its fabric was once well-tailored. Now, its seams barely clung together. Michael allowed himself to slide down the wall until he landed on the dirt road.

"Hey, Mikey," John said. "This ain't all bad."

Michael looked up at John through angry tears.

"Look," John continued. "We can make this a regular gig. Think about it: we can make boatloads of cash and become kings of this town."

He smiled overenthusiastically at Michael, hoping to see a smile in return. With no change in reaction, John continued his persuasion.

"If we make runs for this guy, we won't have to worry about running from those pirates anymore," John said. "We can start over, forget about our worries, and move forward. I mean, come on, Mikey. This place is a goldmine for people wanting to escape their problems, and who better to help them with that than us? We'll move a little cash, a little opium, and live like kings."

Michael wiped his eyes methodically. Standing slowly, a sense of confidence and authority overcame him, a sensation he hadn't felt before.

"No," Michael said calmly. "I won't submit myself to this new kind of slavery. This is bondage to money, to vice, and to whoever Herbert thinks he is. I didn't escape those tunnels to destroy other people's lives. I escaped to return to my own life."

John looked sympathetically at Michael and placed a comforting hand on his shoulder.

"Mikey, that's just not possible," John said. "You have to understand: this is our only choice. Herbert's guys will kill you if you don't do this."

Michael shook John's hand off of his shoulder and stepped back.

"Let them try," Michael said.

Stepping into the middle of the dirt alleyway, Michael began to walk onto the side street. John watched as Michael strolled confidently into the shadows, away from the Scorpion Club, away from guaranteed safety, and into the unknown.

* * *

Even though humidity still lingered, the night air grew colder. Michael wandered aimlessly through side streets and alleyways, unsure of his escape plan, unsure of his next move. He knew Herbert would find him. He knew Herbert would have no issue disposing of him. And for some reason, he didn't care.

Moth flocked to dim light that hung above a saloon door in an otherwise dark alley. Michael gravitated toward the light and walked through the door. As he walked into the shadowy bar, a whiff of cigar smoke and old wood hit him. Stale beer and dirty mop water coated the floor. A few men occupied the small room, scattered at their own tables. This wasn't a rowdy crowd, far removed from the types that liked to dance and holler at the Scorpion Club. This crowd wanted to drink in solitude.

And that's exactly what Michael decided to do.

Walking up to the bar, he sat on a stool and leaned his elbows against the wood, shoving his head into his palms. The bartender wandered over to him slowly and asked him a question in Chinese. Michael didn't understand him, but the implication was clear.

"Whiskey," Michael said.

The bartender nodded. He reached for a bottle of brown liquid and poured some into a short glass. Placing the glass in front of Michael, the bartender held his hand out. The message translated: the bartender wanted Michael's money.

Michael wished he hadn't left the suitcase full of money with

John. He looked at the bartender and shrugged his shoulders. The bartender took the glass of whiskey and pulled it back.

A man at the other end of the bar raised a bill in the air and said something to the bartender in Chinese. The bartender nodded and returned the glass of whiskey to Michael. Nodding toward Michael, the man indicated that he would pay for his drink.

Curious, Michael grabbed his glass and moved to the end of the bar. He sat on the stool next to the man and analyzed him. Michael's usual sense of personal space and tact evaded him, replaced by impatient curiosity.

The man was old, but his bald head hid any trace of gray hair. His deep wrinkles gave the impression of a life well-spent. Sun spots weathered his hands and face, suggesting that the man had spent much of his life outside. He was missing a few molars in his yellowed smile. His eyes were kind, but his stern face projected moral conviction. The man's posture indicated self-control. This surprised Michael; he didn't expect that deduction of a man in a shady bar this late at night.

Michael looked at the man's eyes silently, hoping the silence would prove intimidating. He wanted the man to speak first, but his own suspicion and impatience overcame his plan. Michael held his whiskey glass up and pointed to it.

"Why'd you buy this for me?" Michael asked.

The man stared silently at the whiskey glass before returning his attention to Michael.

"I suppose it doesn't matter," Michael continued. "Thank you. I appreciate it."

Michael lifted the glass to his lips and sipped slowly. He swished it around in his mouth. A surprisingly good bottle of whiskey for such a dingy bar. Looking at the man again,

Michael furrowed his brow inquisitively.

"Do you understand what I'm saying?" Michael said. "Do you speak English?"

The man's face remained expressionless.

"Figures," Michael said to the bartender. "This guy buys my whiskey, the only kind thing a person has done for me in months, and I can't even thank him."

The man smiled. Michael returned his attention to the man and glared at him.

"You do understand me," Michael said. "What's your deal?"

"I wanted to analyze your character," the man said. "I sensed your conflicted energy as soon as you entered the room."

Michael sipped his whiskey again and leaned his elbow against the bar.

"What's your name, old man," Michael asked.

"Lao," he said.

"Michael."

Shaking hands, Michael sunk comfortably into his bar stool.

"So, Mr. Lao," Michael said. "What did you find out about my character?"

Mr. Lao smiled. The wrinkled lines around his eyes creased. He pulled a cigarette from his shirt pocket and lit it. Inhaling smoke slowly, he let it release through his nostrils. Smoke enveloped his head.

"Michael," Mr. Lao said. "Tell me about the problem you're running away from."

"Who says I'm running away from a problem?" Michael said.

Mr. Lao nodded at the whiskey glass. Michael saw his own eyes reflect, bending in the glass. He allowed his head to drop.

"Fair enough," Michael said. "Let's just say I'm in Shanghai against my will and I don't have any more options. No escape plan. There's a powerful man who will be searching for me any minute now. But I don't care. I won't contribute to that vice."

Mr. Lao smiled. Michael sensed that he already knew enough details about the problem before he asked.

"You're the boy running from the captain, aren't you?" Mr. Lao said. "Rough men have been combing the city looking for you. I heard you might have been inducted into service for Herbert."

Michael backed away in fear. Mr. Lao opened his palms and placed them upward, suggesting peace.

"Don't worry, I'm not one of them," Mr. Lao said. "I just heard the news when I came into town to make my regular food delivery. I empty my barrels in the back room and stay for a drink. People at the bar talk. I'm not one of those pirates."

Michael returned to his comfortable, seated position. He sipped his whiskey again to calm his nerves.

"If you want an escape plan that won't compromise your integrity," Mr. Lao said, "come with me. It will be physically and mentally demanding, but I can teach you how to escape with purpose."

Raising his eyebrow with suspicion, Michael glared at Mr. Lao.

"How do I know I can trust you?" Michael asked.

"Would you rather trust Herbert?" Mr. Lao said, nodding toward the door.

Michael looked over his shoulder and saw two men in three-piece suits and fedoras leaning against the wall. One carried a gun in his hand. The other concealed a rope. Michael's heart raced. His pupils dilated. The men stood patiently by the door and waited for Michael to surrender.

"Listen closely," Mr. Lao whispered. "When I pick up my drink, you'll jump over the bar and run through that liquor shelf. It's a secret door. You'll move through the back room and come emerge into an alleyway. There will be an empty barrel. Jump in it and don't move."

Michael opened his mouth to ask a question, but Mr. Lao was already reaching for his drink. Mr. Lao grabbed his glass, stood, and walked toward the door, blocking Michael from view.

Michael leapt over the bar top and landed hard on the wood floor. The suited men dashed toward him. Mr. Lao stuck his foot out, tripping the armed man. Looking at the liquor shelf, Michael shook his head and dashed toward it. A gunshot echoed through the bar. A liquor bottle exploded. Lowering his shoulder, Michael braced for impact. But the shelf flung open, sending Michael into a dark back room.

Shouts and commotion whirled through the liquor shelf, but Michael remained on course. He fumbled through unseen boxes and ran into a table, but eventually, he made his way to the back door. Exploding into the alleyway, he turned left. As promised, he saw three barrels. Quickly scanning the alleyway, he lifted the lid from a barrel, jumped inside, and replaced the lid.

His legs shook. His breathing seemed to echo through the barrel. He felt his heartbeat inside his eardrums.

Michael heard the suited men emerge from the bar's back door. They shouted at each other in Chinese. Their footsteps were erratic. One set of footsteps moved closer and closer to the barrel. Michael held his breath. He tried to stop his heart from beating. He tried to control his shaking hands, but they reverberated more intensely. He knew the barrel was shaking too.

The footsteps stopped. He sensed the suited man next to the barrel. He thought that he could see the man's silhouette.

Then, a loud crash came from around the corner. One man shouted, and two sets of footsteps sprinted around the corner and out of earshot.

Michael exhaled deeply. His heart returned to a regular pace, though his hands still shook.

Then, Michael heard another set of footsteps. Slow this time. Methodical. Confident. As the footsteps approached the barrel, they stopped. Streetlight beams emerged into the barrel as the lid was lifted.

Mr. Lao smiled at Michael, who cowered in the confined barrel.

"Do you trust me yet?" Mr. Lao asked.

Michael stood in the barrel and leaned on Mr. Lao to help him emerge from his hiding place.

"I live a few miles out of town," Mr. Lao said.

Mr. Lao looked down at Michael's bare feet and smiled.

"We'll walk."

Chapter 11

Michael followed Mr. Lao down a small dirt trail. The sun began to rise, red over the dense vegetation that surrounded the path. The city noise had dissipated, replaced by chirping birds and jungle life. Michael perspired exhaustion and humidity through his thin clothes. With swollen feet and hollow eyes, he followed a few steps behind Mr. Lao in silence.

Mr. Lao walked methodically with his hands behind his back. His quiet purpose suggested that he had walked this path many times. He hadn't said much to Michael throughout the entire walk, and Michael had been too tired to spark any form of conversation. There was something mysterious about him, but Michael couldn't pinpoint this sense of mystery. And Mr. Lao's silence hadn't helped Michael's growing curiosity.

Despite the silence and mystery, there was something about Mr. Lao that exuded trust. His eyes portrayed a sense of altruism. Michael just hoped that his instincts were right.

The dirt path led into a small village. Rough awnings hung above rickety wooden shops and shacks that lined the narrow roads. A marketplace served as the center of the village, with wider dirt roads connected shops. Shopkeepers, butchers, and merchants sat in front of their storefronts, which had opened with the sunrise. Michael felt a sense of hospitality.

A river ran along the edge of the village. Women stood ankle-deep in the river washing clothes, while a few men rigged nets to catch fish. Irrigation canals from the river flowed onto wide-open rice paddies.

"This is home," Mr. Lao said. "My farm is up the road."

He pointed to a small wooden farmhouse slightly up the hill. As they approached it, Michael sensed the simplicity, the purpose, the self-reliance. But he also feared that the farmhouse would become his new prison.

Mr. Lao led Michael to the front door, which sat unevenly against the door frame. He unlatched it and removed his shoes, leaving them on a wooden platform outside. Michael walked through the front door. Streaks of sunlight caught dust in the air. The main room contained a small wooden table with three chairs. A fireplace was tucked into the corner, surrounded by a simple stone hearth. Three doors branched off from the main room, but they were closed, leaving Michael to wonder.

Motioning for Michael to sit at the table, Mr. Lao walked to the fireplace. He built a small fire and placed a kettle above it. Soon, water began to boil. Mr. Lao poured two cups of tea and joined Michael at the table.

The warmth of the tea calmed Michael. He felt his feet rest comfortably on the warped floorboards. His back eased its tension. He unclenched his jaw for the first time in months.

"Welcome home," Mr. Lao said.

"Thank you," Michael said.

His voice cracked; he hadn't spoken for a long time. He took another sip of tea to calm his vocal cords.

"Mr. Lao, I appreciate you bringing me here," Michael said, "but I don't understand what I'm doing in your home."

Mr. Lao smiled and set his tea calmly on the table.

"You're here to build yourself into the man you know you can become," Mr. Lao said. "You're here to learn, to work, and to reflect."

Michael raised an eyebrow and leaned forward in his chair.

"I still don't understand," Michael said.

"Michael," Mr. Lao said. "When you walked into that bar last night, I saw something in your eyes that I hadn't seen in a long time. Deep pain. Hopelessness. Despair. I saw in you the same sensations that I once had."

He sipped his tea and returned the cup to the table.

"You see," Mr. Lao continued, "I never had someone to build me back up. I had to figure it out on my own. I made many mistakes in the process. I saw your eyes and recognized an opportunity, a chance for retribution."

Mr. Lao smirked at Michael.

"Now," he said, "tell me what brought such despair into your life."

Michael hesitated, running his hands through his thick beard. He didn't want to reveal his true identity. He didn't want to be sent back to the ship. He didn't want to be delivered to Herbert. But intuition told him to tell the truth, to open his story.

And he did. As the words flowed, tears streamed from Michael's eyes.

Mr. Lao watched patiently. He did not interject. He simply allowed Michael to tell his truth. When Michael finished his story, Mr. Lao stood and poured another cup of tea. Then, he returned to his chair with empathetic eyes.

"It's settled," Mr. Lao said. "You need to hide here, away from Herbert, and you can do that in this village. His reach does not extend this far. Nor does the corruption of the ports."

"But I want to go home," Michael said.

"And you need to return to Portland," Mr. Lao said, "but not yet. It's too dangerous. Even if you make it out of Shanghai, your enemies in Portland will find you. You must return as a new man. Someone who possesses true strength. True wisdom. True understanding."

He smirked again at Michael.

"But, most importantly," Mr. Lao said, "you need some rest."

Mr. Lao went into his bedroom and returned carrying a set of clean clothes. The clothes looked handspun.

"You can wear these," Mr. Lao said. "They belonged to my son. They should fit well enough."

"Anything will be better than these rags I've been wearing," Michael said.

"And you may sleep in that bedroom," Mr. Lao continued. "The other door is mine."

Michael nodded in appreciation toward Mr. Lao. His eyes felt heavy, his heart free, if only temporarily.

"Thank you so much," Michael said. "You have no idea how grateful I am."

"Yes," Mr. Lao said, "I do."

Michael stood and walked toward the bedroom. As he opened the door, he paused and returned his attention to the kitchen.

"Mr. Lao," Michael said, "where does this other door lead to?"

Mr. Lao smiled.

"The farm, of course," he said.

* * *

Sunlight flickered into Michael's closed eyelids, shading his vision in red. He had slept for an entire day. His body needed it. Looking out the window near his bed, he saw nothing but farmland and vertical hills covered in dense jungle. The sound of the nearby river filled the room.

The door creaked open, forcing Michael to open his eyes. Mr. Lao stood in the doorway with a mischievous grin.

"Wake up," Mr. Lao said. "Training begins now."

Michael sat on the edge of his bed and stretched toward the ceiling. His back felt stiff, his legs depleted, and his head pounded. But, somehow, he felt at peace.

As he walked into the kitchen, he saw a small bowl of steamed buns and boiled eggs, accompanied by a glass of water. Mr. Lao sat across from the bowl and read the newspaper silently. Michael ate quickly; his body craved the energy.

"Clean your dish," Mr. Lao said, "and then we work."

Mr. Lao led Michael through the door. The farm spanned endlessly in front of them. Tall, jagged rock islands rose on the horizon, obscured slightly by morning fog. Michael followed Mr. Lao through the small property. The chicken coop sat under a wooden shelter. The rice field sat low on sloped land, while the wheat field spread out on the higher ground. Further back, the land began to run uphill exponentially. Michael stepped onto a terrace that cut into the slope; tomato plants were beginning to flower.

Michael continued to climb, finally stopping on an upper terrace. He turned and looked out over the property and was surprised by how far he had walked. The house looked small in the distance. The sun rose above the forest, bringing humidity and a calming breeze.

"This is where you'll work," Mr. Lao said. "Only if you want to, of course."

"Mr. Lao, I appreciate your kindness, but I'd really like to go back home," Michael said.

Mr. Lao nodded sympathetically.

"And you will, son," Mr. Lao said. "But it's too dangerous for you to return to Shanghai right now. You're lucky you made it out alive after defying a man like Hebert."

Michael's eyes lowered. His mind churned, scouting for ideas.

"Is there another port city I could run to?" Michael asked. "I could book another passage to Portland from there."

"I don't think it's wise for you to return to Portland too soon," Mr. Lao said. "Those who sought to ruin you will do it again."

He paused and scanned Michael's face, trying to read his emotions.

"It would be wise for you to remain here for some time," Mr. Lao continued. "Transform yourself. Search yourself. Find what truly drives you to return. Then, you'll be ready."

Michael lifted his eyes and looked at Mr. Lao. Then, his attention drifted outward, up the hills and into the forest. He felt the presence of nature surround him, a familiar sensation, before his focus returned to the moment.

"I'll hide out here for a little while," Michael said. "I'll help out with your farm. It's the least I can do to repay your kindness and generosity."

Michael sat on a boulder. He tried to see the ocean from his vantage point, but it was too far over the horizon. Tears fell from his eyes. He buried his face in his hands to stop them, but they continued to flow.

Mr. Lao sat on the dirt next to him. He waited silently, letting the bottled grief unleash.

"What's wrong, my friend?" Mr. Lao asked, though he already knew the answer.

"I miss her," Michael said.

"Who?" Mr. Lao asked patiently.

"Emma!" Michael shouted. "She was the love of my life. I was supposed to marry her. I was supposed to start a family. I was supposed to build a house and earn an honest living. And it's all gone."

He held his breath as a tear trickled down his nose. It hung momentarily before falling helplessly in the dirt, where it disappeared.

"It's over," Michael said.

A bird flew across the horizon toward the ocean. Michael wished he could be that bird. He wished he could fly back to Portland and tell Emma that he loved her. He wished he could tell her everything that had happened, that he hadn't missed their date on purpose. He wished he would tell her why he was gone. But he knew she would never find out. Edward would never tell her the truth.

"Eddy," Michael said.

"What?" Mr. Lao said.

Michael stopped crying. His fists tightened and his jaw clenched.

"It was Edward," Michael said. "My best friend. He betrayed me. He sold me into slavery."

"How do you know?" Mr. Lao asked.

Michael was unsure how to answer honestly. He didn't have proof, and his memory of that night was clouded and fading. But still, somehow, he knew. The thought haunted him for months in the darkness of his cell aboard the ship. But the inner struggle to survive pushed the thought away every time it arose. Here, in the safety of this secluded Chinese village, he couldn't hide from it anymore.

"I guess I've always known," Michael said. "I just couldn't bring myself to acknowledge it."

"That's because you're a good person, Michael," Mr. Lao said. "I see it in your eyes, I feel it in your presence."

Michael inhaled deeply. His exhale released tension, released anger. But rage still simmered.

"I was good, Mr. Lao," Michael said. "But I've changed. I want revenge. I want him to suffer like I have suffered. I want to kill him."

Mr. Lao smiled at the rising sun. He stood and breathed in the scents of the forest, the smells of the farm, and the stillness of morning.

"It is not revenge you must seek," Mr. Lao said. "What you must find is balance."

"How can I find balance?" Michael asked.

Mr. Lao smirked as he began to walk down the terraces toward the farm.

"In time, my friend," he said. "In time."

Chapter 12

The rope snapped. The water bucket crashed to the dirt, splashing water all over Michael's leg. With the other water bucket unbalanced, Michael's grip slipped from the shoulder handle, sending the other water bucket toppling to the ground. Michael looked at the mud puddle he had created and shouted in defeat.

Mr. Lao sat on a rock, removing his pipe from his lips to laugh quietly at Michael's struggle.

"I just walked a quarter-mile from the well with those buckets," Michael shouted. "Do I really have to start over?"

"Yes, my friend," Mr. Lao shouted, slapping his knee in laughter. "The goats need water, and I'm getting too old to carry it to them."

Mr. Lao's laugh boomed across the farm.

"And, besides," Mr. Lao continued, "it'll build your strength. Those pirates didn't feed you a thing, you string bean."

Michael picked up the shoulder handle and both buckets. He walked to a workbench underneath the wooden shelter and tied a new rope to the harness. Stomping through the mud puddle, Michael fumed back to the well.

Rain poured from black clouds as Michael slammed the hammer into the nail. Water droplets cascaded from impact.

The fence had fallen down in last night's monsoon, washing it away and lodging it somewhere near the river. Some goats and pigs had escaped, but Michael was able to corral them back to the farm before sunrise.

He was using the remains of the fence to construct a temporary pen for the livestock, but the torrential downpour made it difficult. His long, unkempt hair hung saturated over his eyes.

Once the fence was up, he started on construction of a newer, more stable fence, one that would give the animals plenty of room to roam while maintaining the structural integrity necessary to keep them contained during monsoon season. He was used to rain; it rained every day in the Oregon wilderness. But this was different. It came in waves, waterfalls of rainstorms.

He went into the nearby forest to chop down some trees to begin creating boards. Chopping trees with Mr. Lao's rusty old axe brought Michael back to his comfort zone. He chopped with precision, methodically aiming at his last point of entry in the tree trunk. His shoulders were out of shape; they burned after a few swings. But Michael didn't mind. He fought through the pain, using his burning lungs as fuel to keep chopping. He had found a new tolerance for pain, a new motivation to prove to himself that he was strong, both mentally and physically.

Standing at the workbench, Michael carved boards out of tree trunks. He found this process interesting. He was used to chopping down trees, but he had never seen the next step in the process up close. There was a certain artistry to it, a certain sense of refinement. It was painstaking, but the attention to detail intrigued Michael.

Michael's stomach rumbled. He realized that he hadn't eaten since dinner the night before, and it was already midday. He opened the door to the house quietly to search for some vegetables and dough.

Mr. Lao was still sleeping; the worry of losing his animals had kept him awake after he helped Michael search for his lost livestock. Michael understood. Mr. Lao was old. He had spent a lifetime providing food for his village after losing his own family to disease. He wanted to make sure the farm went on thriving and providing.

The kitchen cabinet snapped in half as Michael opened it. As Michael bent to pick up some wood shards, he felt his feet sink into the old wooden floorboards. The house was old. It was falling apart, rotting from the inside. Dozens of monsoon seasons had withered the house structure.

Moving back to the workbench outside, Michael picked up a board. And then he had an idea.

* * *

With the monsoon season over, Mr. Lao told Michael that he could count on sunshine with light rain for most of the coming season.

Michael constructed the framing near the current, dilapidated house. It took him a few weeks to cut the boards and beams himself, but he was skilled enough with a saw that he created solid framing materials. Mr. Lao helped him stabilize as he climbed on ladders to nail the roof's frame together.

He went into the village to trade for shingles and tar for waterproof adhesive. The wood siding came from trees in the nearby forest, as did flooring for the interior.

Michael connected bamboo to use as plumbing and water pipes underneath the floor and in the kitchen, giving Mr. Lao access to running water from the tank on the roof.

After nearly six months of tireless work, Michael presented the new house to Mr. Lao. Tears of joy, of genuine appreciation, fell from his eyes. He knelt in the dirt in silence.

Mr. Lao displayed more gratitude than Michael could have asked for. His own heart fluttered. It was the first time Michael had felt joy in nearly a year.

But the desire for revenge, for violence, still cursed his thoughts.

* * *

Michael walked along the dirt path that led to the center of town. He passed a few wooden storefronts, waving to a store owner, who eyed Michael with suspicion. Even though he had walked through town at least once each week, Michael still felt like an outsider.

Finally, he found Mrs. Zheng's vegetable stand.

"Good morning, Michael," Mrs. Zheng said, waving her arthritic hand.

"Hello, Mrs. Zheng," Michael said. "How are you today?"

Mrs. Zheng smiled warmly. She appreciated his attempt at the village's Chinese dialect. Michael, however, still felt insecure about his own heavy accent.

"I'm doing alright," Mrs. Zheng said. "Farmers are having a hard season, so I've done my best to help out. But it's not enough."

Michael nodded respectfully.

Nodding toward the bag in Michael's hand, Mrs. Zheng

slapped her palm on the table of her vegetable stand.

"What do we have today?" she asked.

Michael placed the cabbage bag on the table.

"Looks health," Mrs. Zheng said. "I can pay you well for the bag."

Glancing over his shoulder, Michael saw a young girl walking slowly toward the stand, though she kept her distance, probably waiting for Michael to leave.

"You know, Mrs. Zheng," Michael said, "you can just have the cabbage. Use to help out your farmers. We'll bring some more by next week."

Mrs. Zheng nodded in appreciation. As Michael walked away, he watched as the little girl approached the vegetable stand. Mrs. Zheng handed the bag of cabbage directly her and sent her back to her family.

Michael smiled, appreciating the warm sun and the rising humidity.

* * *

The rooster crowed as the sun rose, but Michael was already outside working. Rising before the sun had developed into a habit for Michael. He enjoyed the physical labor. Working the land brought him peace. It quieted his mind, just as it had in the forests outside of Portland.

As he walked into the kitchen to eat breakfast, he saw Mr. Lao sitting at the table sipping tea in silence. Steam rose slowly from his cup. He motioned for Michael to join him at the table.

"How are you feeling today, my friend?" Mr. Lao asked.

"I feel fine," Michael said.

"I mean your mental state, your inner darkness," Mr. Lao

said. "Is it winning? Or are you?"

Michael looked at Mr. Lao with a confused expression, leaning on the table as if moving closer would clarify the question.

"Michael," Mr. Lao said, "it's time to start the next phase of your training, your reconstruction."

Mr. Lao stood and walked outside. Still confused, Michael stood and followed him.

Standing firmly in the dirt, Mr. Lao displayed an intense focus. Michael watched as Mr. Lao moved his arms slowly and methodically. It seemed as if his arms knew where to go before Mr. Lao consciously brought them there. His legs moved in balance with his arms, yet his core remained centered. His eyes were closed, yet he exuded focus. In the midst of this slow, chaotic movement, Michael sensed total control.

"What are you doing?" Michael asked.

Mr. Lao paused and opened his eyes, returning his body to a standing posture.

"Tai Chi," Mr. Lao said.

"What?" Michael asked.

Mr. Lao smiled and waved at Michael to sit on a nearby bench. As Michael sat on the carved wood, Mr. Lao rested on a large stone. Moss covered the rock, bringing life to the barren form.

"Tai Chi," Mr. Lao said, "is an ancient art form. It trains the mind and body to work together for balance. It teaches us to be calm, to be in control while accepting those things we cannot control."

"Is it a dance or something?" Michael asked.

"Not exactly," Mr. Lao said. "It trains the whole person, but it can be used for defense when needed."

Michael laughed.

"Defense?" Michael said. "Like fighting? How is that slow dance going to stop a haymaker?"

Mr. Lao smirked. Placing his hands on his knees, he stood slowly, laboriously.

"Attack me," Mr. Lao said. "I dare you."

Unsure of Mr. Lao's intention, Michael did as he was asked. He moved toward Mr. Lao and threw a punch with his right hand.

Mr. Lao's movement with his hands increased their speed, forcing Michael's hand into the ground, followed by a swift kick to the stomach and a push to the ground. Michael tumbled in the dirt. Dust caked his beard, sending him into a coughing fit.

When he finally regained his bearings, he saw Mr. Lao standing on one leg, swishing his arms methodically in the same formation that took Michael to the ground. But this time, a characteristic smirk graced his face.

"Alright, old man," Michael said. "Teach me."

Tai Chi began each morning before sunrise, accompanied by silence. Michael closed his eyes, balanced his physical and mental presence, and followed humbly in Mr. Lao's shadow.

Mr. Lao served tea and rice for breakfast; simple, yet nourishing.

As they sat at the table, Michael listened to Mr. Lao as he outlined the philosophy that his father and grandfather had taught him many years ago. It was a code that Mr. Lao lived his entire life by. Something Westerners called *Daoism*.

"The world is full of contrast," Mr. Lao said. "The world is always seeking balance. Night and day. Hot and cold. Rain and sun. Oceans and mountains. Fire and water. Moon and sun. Joy and pain. Birth and death. Good and evil."

"Which side are we supposed to choose?" Michael asked. "I like fire when I'm trying to warm up, but I like a drink of water on a hot day."

"It's not about choosing," Mr. Lao said. "It's about allowing nature to find that balance in us."

Michael arched his eyebrows, encouraging Mr. Lao to explain.

"You see, my friend," Michael said, "we are a part of this world, a part of this planet. We are not above it; we are a part of it. The less we try to interfere, the more peace that life will bring to us."

"I don't get it," Michael said.

Mr. Lao wrinkled his forehead, searching for an example to illustrate his point.

"You see this teapot?" Mr. Lao said. "Imagine it is made of pure gold. Let's say I work and work, placing all my effort and focus into obtaining a golden teapot. It would be very glamorous and luxurious, right? It might bring me pride to say that I have this golden teapot. I would find myself becoming attached to it, so much that it might even become a part of my identity."

Michael nodded, still unsure about the direction this analogy was taking.

"But," Mr. Lao continued, "the fact that I have a golden teapot would attract jealousy in others because the equality of all people is now out of balance. So, if someone would come into my house and steal my golden teapot. I would be ruined. My identity and my pride would deflate."

Mr. Lao poured tea from his simple clay teapot.

"The key, my friend," Mr. Lao said, "is to live simply. To

bring extravagance into your life is to invite a jealous thief, who will reset the balance."

Michael nodded in agreement.

"Live simply and forgive those who have wronged us," Mr. Lao continued. "Revenge spirals into more revenge, evil spirals into more evil. But forgiveness restores the balance. It is through forgiveness that we find peace within ourselves."

Chapter 13

Loud coughing and the painful groans lurched Michael from his bed. He listened closely, hearing another coughing fit coming from Mr. Lao's bedroom. Michael leapt from his bed and dashed into Mr. Lao's room.

"Are you alright?" Michael asked.

Mr. Lao shook uncontrollably. Blood trickled from his lips.

"No," Mr. Lao said. "It's time, my friend."

Michael clenched his jaw to fight back tears. *He can't die*, Michael thought. Anguish gripped his body, forcing him to collapse near the bedside.

"I need you to do me a favor," Mr. Lao said, struggling to breath.

"Anything," Michael said.

Mr. Lao inhaled deeply, a task that took most of his energy.

"Walk up to the top terraces at the edge of the farm," Mr. Lao said. "Underneath the engraved stone, you'll find a package. I buried it there last year so that no one would find it except for you."

Michael's mind was spinning.

"You want me to go now?" Michael asked.

"Yes," Mr. Lao said. "Go quickly."

Michael didn't hesitate. He pushed through the door and

sprinted through the farm. He needed to hurry; whatever was in that package could save Mr. Lao.

"Goodbye, my friend," Mr. Lao whispered.

* * *

Michael's lungs burned as he charged up the terraces. Sunlight glistened off the sweat cascading from his brow. His feet stuck into mud that sat stagnant from last night's rain; humidity sweltered as the sun baked the puddles.

Finding the engraved stone, Michael began digging furiously. After a few minutes, his forearms began to seize. He stood up and inhaled heavily, analyzing the holes he had dug without results.

I can't find it, he thought.

He looked purposefully at the stone. In ornate calligraphy, the stone read: *Find balance.* As he read the phrase again, Michael noticed the Chinese characters lined up in an odd way, just slightly off-center. Ironic considering the message. Uncharacteristic of the Chinese writing that Michael had learned from Mr. Lao, he looked closer. The characters lined up to a point. Michael followed that point to the dirt at the corner of the stone. He dug there methodically, patiently.

Finally, his hand struck something that wasn't dirt. Digging around it, he realized it was a large wooden box. He carved his hands around the sides of it and concluded that he couldn't lift it out of the dirt quickly enough. He found the latch and opened the lid. On top of the pile, Michael found a letter.

If you're reading this, the letter read, *it means I have moved on from this life.*

Michael stopped reading. His heart raced. His breathing

ceased. His eyes widened with fear, with a sudden realization that he hoped wasn't true.

Dropping the letter back into the box, Michael dashed down the terraces and across the farm. His feet sloshed through mud puddles. He stomped on grain plants that were almost ready to harvest. He splashed through the edge of a rice paddy. The chickens shouted at him as he leapt over a fence.

Bursting through the door to the house, Michael shouted for Mr. Lao. Entering his bedroom, Michael slowed his pace, afraid of what he would find.

And his fear became a reality.

Mr. Lao was dead.

* * *

After burying Mr. Lao at the top of the terraced hill near the sacred stone, Michael lifted the box out of the ground. He sat in the dirt, leaning against the stone for support. He looked out over the farm and followed the river through its jungle outcropping until it reached the horizon. The red sun hung high in the sky, illuminating the water, sending streaks of dancing light around the horizon.

As he opened the box, he saw the letter; it rested in the same frantic position that Michael had left it. But, somehow, it had settled into the chaos, balancing naturally. The calligraphy was flawless and artistic, characteristic of Mr. Lao himself. It flowed effortlessly, crafted in such a way that balanced the page. Sitting methodically on a stone, Michael wiped the sweat and tears from his eyes as he began to read:

If you're reading this, it means I have moved on from

this life. Michael, it has been an honor and a privilege to have you on my farm. I have come to think of you as a son; I hope you have come to think of me as a father.

For your dedication to me, to this farm, to this village, and to self-improvement, I give you all of my worldly possessions. I know your dream is to return to your home, and for that, I commend you. The farm is yours; you may keep it, or give it to someone that you deem deserving. In this box, I have collected something that will give you more happiness than gold; I have collected what I consider to be the most sacred, useful writings of my life. Some of these are written by me, while most are ancient Chinese texts that contain generations of experiences and knowledge. You are already on the path to becoming enlightened; let these writings guide you the rest of your journey.

I also leave you what little wealth I have. Use this gold to return home. Use this silver to regain the life that was stolen from you. Use this jade to make the world better. Do not use it for revenge, for nature has a way of balancing itself without our interference. Remember, the more simply you live, the more righteous your own balance will be.

With this, I bid you farewell. I thank you for your care, I commend you for your commitment to refinement, and I wish you luck moving forward. It has been an honor to know you.

Sincerely, Lao

Michael looked in the box and found a large pile of gold, silver, jade, and various forms of currency that Mr. Lao must have collected over generations. He found a leather-bound book, which contained writings from Laozi, Confucius, Mencius, and Mr. Lao himself.

He flipped through the book, recognizing some passages that Mr. Lao had often quoted. These passages were interwoven into Mr. Lao's training methods, whether through the simple act of vegetable tending, or the early-morning Tai Chi sessions. These philosophies had now been ingrained into Michael's thoughts, his habits, and his words. He craved balance, nature, and simplicity, but his American upbringing still tugged at him, tempting him back into a life focused on wealth, power, and revenge. A culture, rampant with inequity, beckoned for his return after more than three years.

With the box on his shoulders, Michael returned to the house. He went into the washroom and looked at himself in the mirror. His face was rugged; he was losing the innocence that youth provided. His face had gained a certain refined eloquence, brought on by experience. His hair had grown long, and his beard had grown longer.

Grabbing a knife from the kitchen, Michael returned to the washroom. He cut the fullness of his beard until it was reduced to a stubble. Then, he shaved it carefully, meticulously scraping his skin. He trimmed his hair, beginning with his shoulder-length flow. When he was done, he looked at himself again, hardly recognizing the person he saw returning the stare. His hair was short. His face was clean.

Stepping outside into a light rain, Michael walked to the river. Removing his shoes and shirt, he stepped into the current. Cold water rushed over his feet, sparking invigoration. He took another step into the river, submerging his knees. Finally, he allowed himself to sink below the water. He held his breath and focused on the water's force as it cleansed him. As Michael lifted his head above the water and breathed again, he felt refreshed, revitalized, reborn.

Michael found a small duffel bag from Mr. Lao's closet and stuffed all of his possessions inside: a few changes of clothes, the leather-bound book, and Mr. Lao's wealth. He grabbed the deed to the house, but didn't pack it; he had other plans for the house and the farm. Reaching into a drawer, he removed the wedding ring on the rope necklace, the ring intended for Emma.

Placing the necklace around his neck and under his shirt, Michael stood at the front door. He breathed deeply, calming his mind. He had waited for this moment for three years, but never fully believed it would occur. Part of him wanted to stay in China forever. It provided safety, anonymity. But he couldn't hide from justice any longer. It was time to leave.

As he walked into the village, he saw some familiar faces: shopkeepers, vegetable farmers, fishermen, and kids. Michael walked to Mrs. Zheng's vegetable stand. Her warmness, her genuine kindness, had always made Michael feel welcome.

Michael knew that she had fallen on hard times recently. A dry season had ruined much of the town's staple crop. Yet, despite the hardship, Mrs. Zheng continued to give food freely to those who needed it.

As Michael approached Mrs. Zheng's vegetable stand, he clutched the deed to Mr. Lao's farm in his hand.

"Good afternoon," Michael said in accented Chinese, his Western accent still obvious. "How are you today, Mrs. Zheng?"

"I'm fine, as always, Michael," Mrs. Zheng said.

Michael smiled, concealing the joy he felt for the gift he was about to bestow, yet still hiding his sadness that came with leaving a village that had treated him so well.

"I have a gift for you," Michael said.

He placed the deed to Mr. Lao's farm on the vegetable stand counter. Mrs. Zheng picked it up and analyzed it before widening her eyes. She couldn't believe what she was reading.

"Mr. Lao has passed on," Michael said. "He left the farm to me, and now I'm leaving it to you to continue helping the village with your kindness."

Before Mrs. Zheng could protest, Michael turned and walked down the dirt path, the same dirt path that had taken him to the village three years ago.

Chapter 14

The Shanghai nightlife buzzed as Michael walked into the city. His shoulders ached from the weight of the gold bars in his duffel bag.

He wore plain clothes, a stark difference compared to the suits that most people wore in Shanghai at night. He rubbed his face, still getting used to the exposed skin that had hidden behind his beard for so long. Michael assumed that, since he hardly recognized himself in the mirror, no one in Shanghai would recognize him either.

He found a small shop that exchanged money and precious metals for foreign currency. Considering the number of American business interests in the city, he had no doubt that he could trade gold bars for U.S. dollars.

The exchange room was dark. One man stood behind iron bars at the counter. Cigarette smoke curled around his head.

"What can I do for you?" the man asked.

The man didn't speak with a Shanghai dialect, Michael noticed. Perhaps further north.

"I'd like to exchange these gold and silver bars for U.S. dollars," Michael said. "And this jade."

Michael dumped the metals and jewelry into a pile on the counter.

"And I know the exchange rates," Michael said, "so don't try to screw me."

A smile emerged from behind the money changer's cigarette. After weighing each set of items, he collected the gold, silver, and jade in a large black duffel bag. He disappeared momentarily into a vault, returning with stacks of U.S. currency. He placed the cash on the counter in front of Michael and counted the money audibly. Michael eyed the man as he counted, hoping that the empty threat of knowing the exchange rate would keep him honest.

As the man handed the stack of cash over the counter, Michael opened his own duffel bag and tossed it to the bottom. He realized that this was more cash than he had ever seen in his life. Men worked their entire lives in the forest to acquire a small handful of cash. He couldn't even fathom the possibility of spending all this money in his lifetime.

A wave of paranoia set in, so he covered the cash with his few spare changes of clothes. He thanked the man and left.

As the door closed, the man lifted his telephone receiver and called one of his contacts. Hopefully this contact would give the money changer a cut of his take.

Red neon lights illuminated the dark alleyways and side streets. The sound of the river filled the air, along with the shouts of drunken sailors, villagers, and party-goers. With dinnertime over, the crowd would only grow larger. And louder.

As he turned right into another alleyway, he heard two sets of footsteps approaching. They moved a little more quickly than Michael was comfortable with. He turned and saw two men approaching. One carried a lead pipe, while the other one wielded a knife.

"Give us the bag," one man said to Michael.

Michael smiled and set the bag on the ground in front of him.

"That money changer must have called you as soon as I left," Michael said.

"Doesn't matter," the other man said. "Give us the bag or we'll take it from you ourselves."

Michael's breathing began to quicken, but his mind forced him to calm himself, to find balance. He planted his feet before allowing himself to lighten his posture, to free his mind.

"I'm not going to give you this bag," Michael said. "So, if you're going to fight me for it, go on then."

The two men smiled at each other and tightened their grips on their weapons. One man moved quickly toward Michael and swung with his lead pipe. Michael stepped backward, dodging the pipe. Then, he lurched forward, swiping the man's arm with both hands. Michael's knee dropped down on the man's ankle, breaking it.

As the man screamed on the dirt road, the other man dashed at Michael with his knife. He stabbed toward Michael's stomach, but Michael caught him by the wrist. Punching the man in the stomach, Michael twisted his body and broke the man's arm near the elbow.

Both men wriggled on the ground in pain. Michael picked up his bag, tossed each man a few dollars, and continued his walk through the alleyway. He followed the river; vague memories of the city began to resurface. He crossed a bridge over the river, and then he saw it: The Scorpion Club.

Smirking, he decided to walk by it, just to see how things had changed. As he approached, he realized that he was not dressed for the occasion. He saw men in suits and tuxedos with fedoras and canes. Women wore bright, loose dresses with various types of ornamentation adorning their heads. Vibrant jazz music echoed from the ballroom inside. Michael walked by the entrance and proceeded to the alleyway, to the side door. As he approached, he saw two men walking toward him; one wore a white suit with black edging. There was something familiar about the man. His squat stature, his forced swagger, his ability to fit seamlessly into corruption.

"Hey, Johnny," one man said to the other. "What are we going to do about those deliveries to that British joint across town?"

"We'll just have to force our way in," John said. "That's what Herbert would have done. And, now that I'm in charge, that's what we're going to do."

As the man approached, Michael nodded. He recognized John. He hadn't changed much in three years, though his financial status certainly had. He still walked with the same false confidence that he demonstrated on the ship. He still spoke with the same level of authority on matters that he was ill-suited to discuss. There was no doubt that this was Michael's old cellmate.

John, however, returned the nod to Michael with no recollection or recognition of Michael's identity.

Michael relished in his own anonymity, but his mind still held doubt. He wanted to test his new look, the clean-shaven face, the cropped hair, the simple attire, and the sense of balance. As John walked by, Michael turned and walked toward him.

"Excuse me, gentlemen," Michael said. "I'm looking for a place to have a drink. But I'm not dressed for the occasion at the Scorpion Club. Any idea where a guy like me can find some whiskey?"

John looked at his assistant, and then took two steps toward Michael. He looked him up and down, trying to size up Michael's angle. Michael smelled the alcohol on John's breath. John had three gold teeth on his lower jaw, a change since he landed in Shanghai. But the change that drew Michael in most came from John's eyes. His eye sockets were dark. The whites of his eyes flared. He looked like he hadn't slept in three years, kept awake at night with vice, guilt, and worry.

Finishing his analysis of Michael's threat level, John found Michael to be unthreatening: simple clothes, clear eyes, and open palms.

"Up that alleyway, there's a joint called the Treasure Chest," John said. "You'll find whiskey. You might find even more if you ask the right questions."

John smiled, proud of his innuendo. He elbowed his assistant, who quickly forced a laugh, trying to remain on John's good side.

"Thank you, sir," Michael said.

John tipped his hat, turned around, and disappeared into the Shanghai darkness.

Michael waited for John to evaporate before continuing on his path toward the port. As he neared the edge of town, Michael found a small shop that advertised ticket sales. He walked in and rang the bell at the empty front counter.

Rustling from upstairs turned into frantic footsteps. A light came on behind the counter and an old woman emerged. She rubbed sleep from her eyes.

"What do you want at this hour?" she asked.

Michael put his bag on the floor and nodded humbly.

"I'm sorry for disturbing you this late," Michael said. "I would like to buy a ticket to the United States. To Portland."

The woman looked through her log book, tracing her finger along the chart. Her eyebrows raised as she found the row.

"When would you like to depart?" the woman asked.

"The earliest ticket you have available," Michael said.

The woman's eyes narrowed as she focused on the small print.

"Looks like a ship leaves tomorrow morning at six," she said.

She looked at a clock that hung on the wall near the desk.

"Actually, that's only in a few hours."

Michael saw the price on the ticket, reached into his bag, and paid the woman. To clear his conscience, he left a little extra cash since he had woken her up so late.

The sun rose above the Pacific Ocean as Michael waited on the dock. Though he had been awake for an entire day, he stood by a bench, too energetic to sit down. The ship's horn sounded. Michael grabbed his duffel bag and walked up the ramp to the medium-sized steamer.

A sailor stood at the end of the ramp and held out his hand for Michael's ticket.

"Going to Portland?" the sailor asked.

Michael smiled, handed his ticket to the sailor, and gripped his duffel bag tightly.

"I sure am."

Chapter 15

Michael's cabin was small. It featured a single bed and, when he stretched across it, his ankles hung over the edge. He placed his spare clothes in the small dresser drawers and slid his duffel bag far underneath his bed. He set Mr. Lao's leather-bound book of writing on the compact desk, which faced the small porthole window. Michael's room was near the bottom of the ship, so his window gave him a close view of the ocean's waves.

After he settled himself into his room, he made time for meditation and Tai Chi. At first, he resented the difficulty of practicing Tai Chi in such a confined area, but he soon appreciated the challenge.

As his room filled with light, he heard the ship's horn echo through the ship, signaling its departure. Michael wanted to see the port that had changed the course of his life; he had never seen it in the daylight. He left his cabin and walked down the narrow hallway, passing dozens of small rooms as he moved. Some room doors were open, while some looked uninhabited. Finally, he reached the end of the corridor and climbed the stairs. His feet clinked on the grated metal staircase, triggering memories of his last time on a ship.

The morning air felt crisp, refreshing Michael's growing

sense of entrapment. He walked toward the railing and looked out over the port. Wooden docks lined the bay. Guard stations, trading posts, and customs booths littered the docks. Hundreds of small fishing boats bounced on their ties and buoys. Near the other end of the harbor, Michael saw a large steamer that looked familiar. He inhaled deeply through his nose and held his head high, proud of his escape.

The ship began to move, weaving through the maze of buoys and fishing boats as it navigated its way out of the harbor. Michael turned and walked toward the middle of the deck. Finding an unoccupied bench, he sat down and allowed the humid sea breeze to cleanse his spirit.

Suddenly, a high-pitched wail pierced through the silence, followed by loud cheers. As Michael listened, the high-pitched sound became melodic, soothing, exciting. The trumpet grew louder. A simple percussion drove the music. Not from a drum set, but from something more basic; one source of rhythm. Someone began to sing over the trumpet. Not lyrics, but rhythmic vocals. Almost a percussion of its own. It seemed paradoxical; spontaneous music, yet well-rehearsed.

Michael stood and wandered toward the sound. He saw three men near the railing performing this music, this joy to the soul. One man stood and wailed on his trumpet, while another stood near him, singing and making beautiful melodies from non-lyrical vocals. The singer seemed to feed off of the trumpeter. Or maybe the trumpeter fed off of the singer. It seemed so organic. The drummer sat on a wooden box and played a complex rhythm with his palms, using various parts of the box to enact new pitches.

This was jazz, but not the jazz that Michael was used to hearing on the radio or in a club. This was something new.

A small crowd gathered and bopped along to the music. Not one for crowds, Michael distanced himself and leaned against the railing, nodding his head to the rhythm. He couldn't help it.

After a few songs, the band stopped playing. The crowd dissipated. The trumpeter, the singer, and the drummer strolled toward Michael, toward the back of the ship.

"You guys were incredible," Michael said as they passed.

The men looked at each other, unsure of how to respond. The trumpeter decided to stop and reply, encouraging the other two members to do the same.

"Why, thank you, sir," the trumpeter said.

"Are you the on-board entertainment?" Michael asked.

The trumpeter smiled.

"No, sir," he said. "We're just on our way back to the States from Shanghai. We played at a few clubs here."

"You came all the way to Shanghai to play in a few clubs?" Michael asked.

"Sure did," the trumpeter said. "They paid us for it, so why not?"

Michael shrugged his shoulders, seeing the point in the trumpeter's statement. He turned to walk away with his band mates, but he paused and returned his attention to Michael.

"Say, we're going to play some cards down in the common room later on when we get a little ways from shore," the trumpeter said. "See you down there around nine?"

Michael nodded casually.

"See you there," he said.

Moving toward the back of the ship, Michael leaned against the railing. He saw Shanghai's shores glistening in the morning sunlight. Vegetation blocked the city itself from view. A slow smile crept onto Michael's face as Shanghai began to fade away into the horizon. Finally, he had escaped.

* * *

After a simple dinner of rice and vegetables, Michael moved down to his cabin. He heard laughter at the end of the hallway, so he passed his cabin door and moved toward the laughter. He turned the corner and walked into the common room.

The trumpeter saw Michael walk in and offered him a chair between the drummer and the singer.

"Want to get in on some poker?" the trumpeter asked. "One dollar buy-in."

Another game of poker in the depths of an iron ship, Michael thought.

"I'd love to," Michael said.

Michael placed a dollar on the table and the singer gave him chips. The drummer dealt five cards to each player. Michael concealed a smile as he looked at his cards: three tens, a jack, and a queen.

"You know, you might get killed for a thing like this back home in the States," the singer said.

"A thing like what?" Michael asked.

The drummer slapped his knee and laughed.

"For playing cards with a couple Black fellas like us," the singer said.

Michael paused. The silence was palpable. He hadn't even thought about it; maybe his time in China had loosened the grip of America's caste system.

"But we're not in the States, are we?" the trumpeter said, laughing.

Cracking a smile, Michael placed the jack and the queen down on the table. The drummer dealt him two more cards: a four and a nine.

"You know," Michael said, "I grew up with a lot of Black folks."

The drummer looked at Michael in disbelief. The trumpeter waved off the comment and returned to his cigarette.

"Man, you're just trying to butter us up so you can take our money," the singer said. "Typical white man."

"I'm serious," Michael said. "My parents were Irish immigrants. We lived in a neighborhood in North Portland with other Irish immigrants and Black folks. Most of them moved to Portland from places like Mississippi. To work in the shipyards, I guess."

The trumpeter nodded, taking another drag from his cigarette.

"So what?" the singer said. "Just because you live around a couple Black families, you think you know us? You think you understand our pain?"

A wave of guilt ran through Michael's nerves. He dropped his head, ashamed of his own assumptions, ashamed that the stain of America's caste system hadn't completely washed away. Maybe it never would.

"No," Michael said, "and I don't know if I ever could."

"Have you ever been treated like an outcast before?" the trumpeter asked.

Michael nodded, reflecting on his own walks through Mr. Lao's village, his own sprints through Shanghai.

"Now, imagine being treated like that in your own home," the trumpeter continued, "the home you built with your bare hands."

Unaccustomed to this honesty, a type of candor that could only take place off of America's shores, Michael's face sunk along with his spirit. For the first time, he began to see his own pain reflected in his own homeland, in his own city, mystified that he hadn't paid attention to it before this simple game of cards.

"I read a book by an Irish guy once," the trumpeter said. "James Joyce. You know him?"

Michael shook his head, unfamiliar with the name.

"Man, I thought all you Irish folks knew each other," the trumpeter asked, smirking. His raspy voice reverberated with the cigarette smoke he simultaneously released. "You from North Portland?"

"I am," Michael said. "Near the shipyards."

"I've got a cousin who used to live there," the trumpeter said. "Never made it out there myself, though."

Michael nodded in acknowledgement; the name sounded slightly familiar.

"Maybe he lived in the tenement across the street," Michael said. "The last name rings a bell. Does he play the trumpet like you?"

The trumpeter slapped his knee with his cards and grinned. Cigarette smoke wafted from his nose as he laughed.

"He sure does," the trumpeter said.

"But not as well as you, though," the singer said, throwing his head back in laughter.

Michael couldn't help but laugh with them. He placed his four and nine on the table; the drummer dealt him two more cards. The four men placed their last bets and showed their cards.

Scoring two fives on his last deal, Michael showed a full

house. The drummer didn't show his cards, admitting defeat. The singer showed three sixes, still admitting defeat. The trumpeter inhaled deeply, dramatically folding his cards on the table one-by-one. Four kings. The trumpeter feigned apology and collected his chips from the center of the table.

"Nice one," the drummer said.

The singer shuffled the cards; it was his turn to deal. He dealt each man five cards and lit a cigarette. He offered one to Michael, who took one graciously.

"So, what part of the States are you heading back to?" Michael asked.

"Harlem," the singer said.

"You all are from New York?" Michael asked.

"Not exactly," the singer said. "The three of us are from New Orleans, actually. But Harlem has a real vibrancy going on right now. All these Black artists, poets, dancers, and writers have gravitated there. It's a real happening place. We couldn't be left out of it."

"Got a guy name Armstrong out there," the trumpeter said. "I hear he plays a mean trumpet like me. Maybe we can bring that New Orleans sound up North and make it stick."

The singer dealt cards to each of the men again.

"Well," Michael said, "maybe we'll hear about you guys in a few years. If you ever tour in Portland, look for me at your show."

"The Solomon Band," the trumpeter said. "You'll see our name in lights one day."

He laughed and placed two more cards down for the final round of betting. As Michael placed his cards down, he noticed the drummer eyeing him. His stare was intense.

"What's on your mind?" Michael asked the drummer.

114

"You've got something in you," the drummer said. "I see it in your eyes, in your soul. Something is weighing on you. You're fighting a battle."

Michael picked up his cards and attempted to place together his best hand.

"Aren't we all," Michael said.

* * *

Michael sat at his desk. The leather-bound book sat open, though Michael's eyes were closed. One of Mr. Lao's sayings resonated in his mind: *Allow nature to restore balance and good fortune will grace your future.*

The premise seemed simple. Let nature take its course. If Edward was responsible for ruining Michael's life, then nature should ruin Edward's life in return, leaving Michael free from the spiritual weight of enacting vengance.

But the desire to seek revenge for betrayal haunted Michael's thoughts, his dreams. This desire had permeated his thoughts for three years, and this seed had begun to sprout. Every attempt to push the desire for vengeance out of his mind had failed. Tai Chi, meditation, reading, and sleep subdued it, but the desire remained.

Maybe the only way to rid himself of the temptation for revenge was to push nature's course along, to control the direction that nature needed to move in order to restore balance.

Looking through his porthole window, Michael opened his eyes. He saw land on the horizon, so he left his room and climbed the stairs. Moving toward the railing, he watched as the Oregon Coast moved closer.

Michael clutched the wedding ring around his neck. The ship thrashed as it charged into the notorious Columbia River bar. It pushed upriver before moving south into the Willamette River.

And then he saw it through the evening fog. The red cage of the Broadway Bridge. The warehouses. The cars and horses. The cobblestone and dirt roads. The train station. The smell of light rain on concrete.

Michael had finally returned to Portland.

Chapter 16

Street lights flickered on as the sunlight faded. Rainy mist clung to the ground. Walking across the Broadway Bridge, Michael hitched a ride on the back of an open automobile, driven by someone making a grain delivery from the mill near the river. The driver asked a few questions, but Michael had only one thing on his mind: his next move.

The vehicle sputtered into North Portland, moving parallel to the Willamette River's train tracks. The driver told Michael to jump off; he refused to drive his automobile any further into that part of town. Michael thanked the driver, finding amusement and offense in the driver's fear of Michael's old neighborhood.

With his duffel bag slung on his back, Michael walked a few blocks up Russell Street until he got to Mississippi Avenue. His old tenement neighborhood stood just three blocks further. He figured the Irish tenement would be a good place to start. He had family there. At least he used to. Three years had passed.

As he walked on the cobblestone street, he saw the red sign for the Bald Eagle. He paused and looked at the two-story brick building; vines covered most of the exterior. If he was going to reconnect with an old contact, he knew he could find one in here.

During his teenage years, Michael and his cousin, Patrick, used to come to the Bald Eagle to drink beer and play cards. They got into their fair share of fist fights here. This was a lawless side of town.

Michael opened the doors and scanned the room. Dim lights reflected off the red brick. The bar room seemed smaller than he remembered. A few tables were placed in the small room, along with two barstools that stood at the short bar. One man sat at the bar, while the tables remained empty.

A large man with a dark moustache stood behind the bar top. Michael approached slowly, still scanning the room for anyone that looked familiar. As Michael approached the bar, he caught his reflection in the mirror. He still didn't recognize himself.

"What'll it be?" the bartender asked.

"I'll have a whiskey," Michael said.

The bartender threw his head back and laughed. He looked at Michael with disbelief and superiority.

"Son, I don't know where you think you are," the bartender said.

Michael raised an eyebrow and looked sideways at the man sitting at the bar who was laughing too.

"I don't get the joke," Michael said.

"You must have just gotten off the boat from Ireland, kid," the bartender said. "Prohibition is in effect. You can't just walk up and order a drink anymore. That'll get you arrested, and that'll get me shut down."

"Prohibition?" Michael asked.

"Yes, sir," the bartender said. "I don't like it, but that's the new law of the land. No more alcohol. Now, we just serve food."

Michael rolled his eyes and returned his attention to the mirror.

"Water, then," Michael said.

The bartender poured a glass of water and placed it on the bar. Michael grabbed it and went to a table and sat down.

Soon, the man sitting at the bar stood up and walked over to Michael's table. He pulled out a chair and sat down.

"You a cop?" the man asked.

Michael laughed, nearly choking on his water.

"Me?" Michael said. "A cop? Not a chance."

"Good," the man said. "You don't strike me as a cop, but I have to ask."

Michael leaned into the table. The confrontation struck his curiosity.

"Walk up to the bartender and ask him to *see the library*," the man said.

Reclining in his chair, Michael read the man's face. He seemed honest enough. Corrupt, maybe, but honest enough. Standing, Michael walked to the bar.

"I'd like to see the library," Michael said.

The bartender eyed Michael. He paused, looked at the other man, and then nodded to Michael. He moved out from behind the bar and walked into a small hallway. Michael followed. At the end of the hallway, Michael saw a bookshelf.

"You might be interested in *The Count of Monte Cristo*," the bartender said.

The bartender returned down the dark hallway and disappeared. Michael looked at the bookshelf. He found *The Count of Monte Cristo* on the middle shelf. As he pulled the book, he noticed that it seemed heavier than a standard novel. He pulled with additional strength. A latch unhooked and the bookshelf popped off the wall, releasing a wave of sounds into the hallway. Michael swung the bookshelf open like a door.

He walked into the room behind the bookshelf and recognized it immediately as the Bald Eagle from his youth. An attendant quickly closed the door behind him. Bright lights illuminated the crowd. A small jazz band played in the back corner, where dozens of people danced in a way that Michael had never seen. Small wooden tables were scattered across the room's old wooden floors, packed with the neighborhood's familiar demographics: Black and Irish. People sat with drinks and played cards. A large bar lined the entire side wall.

Approaching the bartender, Michael ordered a whiskey. The bartender poured a small glass and slid it to Michael. Grasping the short glass, Michael leaned against the bar and watched the crowd, scanning it for any trace of familiarity.

The band in the corner played a slow melody over a swinging drum beat. The singer crooned on the microphone.

After the song ended, the singer stepped back, took a drink from his glass of brown liquor, and stepped to the microphone again.

"Alright, now," the singer said in a raspy, soothing tone, "y'all ready to turn things up?"

The crowd cheered. More people stood from their tables and made their way to the dance floor.

"Now, where I'm from, down in New Orleans" the singer continued, "we're starting to push the tempo. We're going to try something a little new out on you, if that's alright."

The crowd erupted again. The singer nodded to the crowd, tipped his hat, and then turned to the drummer to begin the count. The bass, snare, and hi-hat kicked at a rapid rhythm with a serious swing. Trump notes floated intermittently through the beat. And then, the singer started to scat.

Dancers twirled and grooved on the dance floor, fueled by liquor and freedom. Michael was transfixed. He wanted to join the crowd and dance. He felt a pull. But before he could move away from the bar, he noticed a change in balance. The volume at a nearby table began to rise. Soon, shouting erupted as someone tossed a poker hand at another player. A bearded man stood, throwing his chair back in anger.

"You're a cheat!" a man shouted.

A red-headed man stood to defend himself. His cheeks flared red against his white, freckled skin.

"Am not!" the accused man said. "You're just not very good at poker."

The bearded man threw a punch that hit the red-headed man square in the jaw. The red-headed man shook his head and returned with a punch to the beard man's ribs. The bearded man jabbed at the red-headed man, but he missed and knocked the drink out of a man's hand who stood near the table. Punches were thrown. A chair broke. A bottle crashed to the floor.

Michael watched in amusement as the red-headed man slipped out of the fight and stood against the bar in a corner, unseen by the three men engaged in fighting each other. He placed a cap on his head to further disguise himself. The bartender stepped in and separated the brawlers, who finally returned to the respective tables.

Finishing his whiskey, Michael ordered two more and walked to the red-headed man, placing one whiskey glass in front of him. The red-headed man looked at Michael with caution.

"Thanks," the red-headed man said. "What's this for?"

"To celebrate," Michael said.

"Celebrate what?" the red-headed man asked.

"Your cousin's return home."

* * *

Cigarette smoke lingered in the light above the corner booth. Patrick removed his cap, ruffled his red hair, and placed the cap further back on his head. He looked at Michael, still trying to wrap his mind around his clean-shaven, lean appearance. He took another sip of whiskey and leaned in further, captivated by Michael's story.

"I thought you were dead," Patrick said. "Everyone did. Everyone *does*."

"I should be dead," Michael said. "I'm lucky I got out."

Michael leaned back in his seat, realizing that this was the first time he had recounted his entire story.

"So," Patrick said, "you think it was Edward who did this to you?"

"I'm certain," Michael said. "I tried to push the idea out of my mind for three years. I've thought of every other possibility. But I've come to the full realization that my best friend betrayed me."

Patrick tipped his cap in unfortunate agreement.

"You've always got your eyes and ears open," Michael said. "What have you heard about Eddy?"

"You really want to know?" Patrick asked.

Michael nodded and braced himself for the truth.

"Well, the word around town is that he's on the rise," Patrick said. "Soon after you disappeared, he left the forest and returned to the city. Somehow, he got a lot of money and

122

was able to buy some influence around town. I'm not sure exactly what he does or how he's connected. I do know that he's in close with the police chief."

Michael slammed his fist on the table. He felt his temperature rise and tried to calm his breathing.

"You know where he got that money?" Michael said. "By selling me off."

Patrick took a swig of his whiskey and shook his head in bewilderment.

"Well, cousin," Patrick said. "What are we going to do about it?"

Chapter 17

Rain poured from low clouds, covering downtown in gloom. The afternoon sun struggled to produce any sort of light. Water rushed down the street. Business people covered their heads with umbrellas and newspapers as they walked.

Michael stood motionless underneath an awning in front of a coffee shop. The door to Quimby's hadn't opened in an hour, but Michael waited. Patrick had informed Michael that Edward made a regular stop at Quimby's to pick up a payment.

As the rain began to slow, Michael reached into his coat pocket and clutched the knife, making sure it was still there. It weighed heavy in his hand, knowing that he would have to use it soon enough.

He also knew this would likely get him arrested, especially since Edward had connections with police. Patrick had only heard rumors. But his contacts with the police chief would force Michael's swift arrest.

But Michael didn't care. No jail or execution would stop him from exacting revenge. For three years, he had waited for this moment. He plotted his revenge in his cell on the ship to Shanghai. He dreamed about his attack while he hid in the back room at the bar. He planned his revenge while he wandered the streets of Shanghai, waiting to be killed by a notorious opium dealer. And he crafted his plan for revenge during long days on Mr. Lao's farm.

Sorry, Mr. Lao, Michael thought.

He pushed the thought of nature's balance from his mind. Teaching of forgiveness swelled in his heart; Michael forced the feeling from his body. Revenge left no room for compassion.

Quick footsteps splashed in puddles across the street. A familiar voice echoed around the corner. And then he appeared.

Edward's face sparked anger in Michael, a desire to rob him of the life he had stolen. His wide-brimmed fedora. His three-piece suit. His shiny, leather shoes. And that obnoxious smirk that hid his transgressions.

Michael grasped the knife in his pocket and walked briskly across the street. Edward stood in the doorway, apparently waiting for someone. He would never see Michael coming. Even Patrick hadn't recognized his own cousin.

The knife felt heavy in his hand as Michael began to draw it out. Edward was close. Just a few steps away.

And then he heard it. The sweetest voice in the world. The sound of a bluebird singing in a pine tree, whistling soft notes of pure joy. A voice that could make all wars stop.

Emma.

She rounded the corner. Michael shoved the knife in his pocket and tucked his face into his petticoat collar. He couldn't change his path without drawing attention, so he walked directly by Edward, avoiding eye contact with his enemy. And then he breezed by Emma; her smell made his heart flutter.

Michael crossed the street again and leaned against a newspaper stand. He watched as Emma found Edward waiting in the doorway.

"Oh, my dear Edward," Emma said. "I'm sorry I'm late."

"Not a problem, darling," Edward said.

Edward kissed Emma on the cheek. Michael lost his will to breath. His heart wrenched. He clutched his stomach, unable to turn his gaze away from the disaster unfolding before his eyes. Emma reached for Edward's hand and the couple strolled into Quimby's together. The door shut slowly behind them.

Michael didn't command himself to run. He just ran. He sprinted through puddles as he gasped for air. He ran as fast as he could, not caring where his legs took him. He needed to move as far from Emma as he could. He found himself dashing across the Broadway Bridge; its red cage encased Michael as he stopped in the middle, finally running out of air.

He looked over the edge. The Willamette River's waters rushed below. He could jump. He could simply jump and float to the bottom and no one would ever know. The cold would probably force him to inhale water and cause him to drown. To sink.

But what would that do? That would give Edward the victory that he already assumed he took from Michael.

Inhaling through his nose, he slowed his breath. He slowed his heart rate. He calmed himself and found his center. He attempted to regain his balance. Standing on one leg, he swayed his arms in a habitual Tai Chi motion. Mr. Lao's mantras echoed faintly in his mind.

Finding calmness, Michael regained control over his raw emotions. He watched a small boat float along with the river. The natural force of the river moved the boat, but the man's oar easily guided the craft in the proper direction.

Michael strolled lightly across the bridge, emerging back into his old neighborhood, back into the tenements. He needed support. And he needed a plan.

Fog had settled along the river near the rail yards in North Portland. The Bald Eagle appeared empty, aside from the bartender. Michael approached, relayed the password, and walked through the hidden bookcase. Patrick sat in the back corner booth as planned.

"Alright, Mikey," Patrick said in a low voice. "Is he dead?"

Michael shook his head.

"I couldn't do it," Michael said. "He was right there, exactly where you said he'd be. And I couldn't do it."

"Why not?" Patrick said. "He's the guy who ruined your life. He took everything from you."

Michael lowered his head, but raised his eyes at Patrick.

"Emma was with him," Michael said.

Patrick leaned back in his seat. He tipped his hat up and ran his hand down his face.

"Did you know they were together?" Michael asked.

Sipping his whiskey, Patrick avoided eye contact with his cousin. Finally, conviction forced him to look at Michael.

"You know, Mikey," Patrick said, "I've heard some rumors. Rumors that she was devastated when you disappeared. Rumors that you ran away with another woman. Rumors that she searched the streets for you for months. Edward was there to console her, to comfort her."

"Patrick," Michael said, "what do you know?"

"A reliable source told me that they're engaged to be married," Patrick said.

Michael sunk into his seat; the puffed leather enveloped him. He sank further, weighed down by the knife in his pocket. He looked at the glass of whiskey in front of him. He reached for it, but as his hand touched the glass, he recoiled. He felt compelled to maintain balance, to maintain control.

"This changes everything," Michael said.

"How do you mean?" Patrick asked.

"I can't just kill Edward in cold blood anymore," Michael said. "My goal has always been Emma. My goal will always be Emma. I can't just kill her fiancé and then ask for her hand in marriage."

The band played loudly across the room, but silence surrounded the table. The jazz music seemed but a faint echo to Michael. Patrick searched his cousin's face, looking at glimpses of the past three years.

"A new plan then," Patrick said, breaking the silence.

Michael smiled and tipped his cap.

"A new plan," Michael said. "What have you been able to dig up on Edward?"

* * *

Patrick and Michael had always been close. They were first cousins, but they had grown up in the same tenement building. Separated by just a few months, the Sullivan cousins ran around North Portland together as kids. They caused their fair share of trouble, but it was mostly harmless. Throwing rocks at passing trains. Swimming in the river. Sneaking onto ships in the port.

Michael's brothers joined often, until they drifted into more nefarious activities. He knew that two of his brothers were in jail. He hadn't heard from the other one since secondary school; he had probably escaped in hopes of joining the Great War in Europe and found distraction along the way. Patrick was the only family member who stayed loyal, who treated

Michael with any kind of humanity.

Patrick accompanied Michael to elementary and secondary school. As they reached adulthood, they frequented the Bald Eagle and other neighborhood establishments that welcomed undesirables like themselves. When Michael took the logging job in the forest, Patrick lost a moral influence. Michael always brought a set of values and ethics that Patrick admired and strived to uphold.

When Michael disappeared, Patrick kept a close watch on Michael's situation. He suspected foul play; he knew Michael wouldn't just leave without one last drink at the bar. And he knew that Michael loved Emma too much to abandon her the way it appeared.

So, Patrick used the connections he had made over the years at bars, poker rooms, construction sites, the shipyards, and pickpocket dealings. He gathered information about Michael's disappearance. But, with key pieces of information missing, he wasn't able to complete the story. However, now that Michael was back, his wealth of information about the city's underworld began to piece itself together. And, since Michael's return from the dead, Patrick had reached out to some of those contacts again to make more connections.

Patrick figured out that Edward made his money from bootlegging. He capitalized on the forbidden desire for alcohol when Prohibition started. Edward gave a solid percentage of his monthly earnings to Portland's police chief, William Cooper. According to a contact at Patrick's regular poker room, Cooper ran a speakeasy out of his own basement in Southeast Portland. Just for fun; he didn't need the money after the cut he took from the big bootleggers in the city.

Cooper would arrest bootleggers, pose for a picture with the captured liquor, and then dispose of the liquor down the sewer drain. Meanwhile, one of Eddy's boys would sit underneath the drain with a barrel and reclaim the liquor. In addition to his bribe, Cooper got to keep some of the liquor, and that's what he served in his own speakeasy. The pictures were printed in the press and Cooper looked like he was tough on crime. All the while, he was getting rich off bribery and drunk on illicit booze.

"So, Eddy is paying off the most powerful cop in the city," Michael asked.

"It appears so, cousin," Patrick said.

"What do we do about it?" Michael asked.

Patrick smiled. Michael had seen this smile before. It was the type of smile that indicated mischief. The type of smile that acknowledged danger, but pushed forward anyway.

"Let's pay a visit to a speakeasy in Southeast Portland," Patrick said. "I know a gal who works over that way. I bet she can get us in."

Chapter 18

Streetlights attempted to pierce the fog as a humid chill fell over Southeast Portland. Michael flipped his petticoat collar up and buried his neck into the wool. His beard used to provide warmth against the Northwest chill; he still wasn't used to his clean-shaven face. Patrick pulled his cap tight over his head. They walked silently. The sound of their shoes echoed off the houses that lined the narrow street. There was no need to speak. They knew the plan.

As they moved down 40th Avenue, they saw a couple dressed in fine evening attire cross the street into the light, looking cautiously over their shoulders as they moved. The woman wore a dazzling dress and a jeweled headband, while the man wore a tailored suit with a wide-brimmed fedora.

"We must be in the right neighborhood," Patrick said.

The couple disappeared into an alleyway.

"There it is," Patrick said.

Michael and Patrick turned into the alleyway, passing rickety wooden fences as they walked. They came to a driveway that led to a house's side door. Patrick hesitated, looking at Michael for reassurance. With a nod from his cousin, Patrick knocked on the door. A slot slid open, revealing a pair of eyes.

"Who are you here to see?" a deep voice said through the

door.

"We're here to see the Czar," Michael said.

"The Czar is dead," the voice said.

Michael felt his nerves fire in his legs. He was ready to run if the next phase of the password didn't work. Taking a deep breath, he continued.

"Long live the revolution," Michael said.

The slot slammed shut. Michael looked at Patrick, unsure if the password had worked.

Then, a series of locks clanked and unbolted, and the door swung open. Michael and Patrick entered the dark opening. The guard slammed the door shut behind them, locking it, trapping any retreat. They walked nervously down a dark staircase. The wooden steps creaked underneath their feet. They reached the bottom of the staircase, landing firmly on cracked cement. A black door blocked their progress. Michael looked to Patrick, unsure whether or not he should open the door. Turning back was not an option, so he turned the doorknob.

A light drum beat and jazzy saxophone floated through the air. Low lights illuminated the basement. Lively chatter filled the room. A few wooden tables scattered across the floor around a pool table. A bar stood in the corner; it rested on wheels so it could be hidden and stored easily.

Michael followed Patrick; this was his world. Projecting a false confidence, Patrick moved smoothly through the crowd.

"Alright," Patrick said quietly, "our first move is to grab a drink at the bar and sit casually. We need to blend in."

They walked to the bar and ordered two Manhattans, which the bartender poured with ease. Spotting two open stools in the back corner, the Sullivan cousins sat and observed.

A pool game was ending. The two men placed their cues on the table and walked to the bar, so Patrick stood and picked one up. He motioned to Michael to follow. Racking the balls, Patrick watched the unsuspecting tables around him. He wasn't sure exactly what he was listening for, but he needed to remain aware.

As the lazy pool game faded, Patrick saw a familiar face enter the speakeasy. He knew she would be here. He knew she frequented this speakeasy. Patrick also knew that she was in with Cooper's usual crowd; she had useful information. She walked arm-in-arm with a well-suited man. Probably a banker. Maybe an off-duty cop. Patrick smiled and returned his attention to the pool game. He didn't want to appear too suspicious.

The game finished. Patrick placed the cues back on the table and looked at his cousin.

"Say, why don't you go order another round of Manhattans," Patrick said.

"But I haven't finished this one," Michael said.

Patrick looked at Michael with a sense of urgency. Michael didn't know what Patrick had planned, but he decided to trust his street-smart cousin. Michael leaned against the bar and ordered another round of drinks. Buying time, he made small talk with the bartender as he watched Patrick.

Moving smoothly through the growing crowd, Patrick waited for the woman to distance herself from the man she came with. Then, he made a strategic bump into her. Looking over his shoulder, he lifted his eyebrows with a facade of excitement.

"Josephine," Patrick said, "I haven't seen you in ages, my dear. How are you?"

She kissed Patrick on the cheek, holding her cigarette elegantly. Her long, white gloves contrasted against her black skin.

"I'm doing just fine, Patrick," Josephine said, batting her long eyelashes. "What kind of mischief have you been getting into lately?"

"You know me," Patrick said. "Say, this is a pretty swanky joint. Do you come here often?"

"To Cooper's speakeasy?" Josephine said. "Of course I do. I can't go to any legitimate joints downtown. But down here, in speakeasies like this, I can be whoever I want. Is it your first time here?"

"It sure is," Patrick said.

Patrick paused, mustering the courage to ask the next question. He trusted Josephine, but he didn't trust her that much, mostly because of his own past indisgretions. Regardless, he needed to test her. He needed to see where her loyalties stood.

"You know, Josephine," Patrick said. "I walked by the old mill the other day. Remember when we finished that bottle of wine and spent the night in the mill tower?"

Josephine blushed, lightly slapping Patrick in the arm. She looked around to make sure no one else heard the comment. Patrick smiled and feigned embarrassment.

"Speaking of old memories, I was talking to a friend of mine the other day about an acquaintance," Patrick said. "Edward Bishop. Have you heard of him?"

"Sure I have," Josephine said. "It's hard not to recognize that name when you run in Cooper's circle. Wasn't he friends with your cousin, Michael?"

"He was," Patrick said.

Patrick nodded and feigned sadness, assessing his next

conversational maneuver. He wasn't sure how far he could press her. He wasn't sure if he maintained a high position. Deciding to take the risk, he pushed forward casually, masking his urgency.

"You know, I never actually had the chance to meet Edward," Patrick asked. "What do you know about him? And how's he connected to this swanky new speakeasy?"

"Typical Patrick Sullivan," she said. "Always trying to collect gossip."

Patrick's lungs deflated, but he maintained a calm facade. She was into him.

"You know me," he said coyly.

Josephine smirked and rolled her eyes. Then, she looked around to make sure she wasn't in range of her date, or any other familiar ears. With an airy smirk, she dove in.

"Eddy is a real man about town," Josephine said. "In fact, he's becoming one of Portland's richest bachelors. Bootlegging, of course."

Patrick raised his eyebrows curiously, but not overbearingly. He didn't want to appear overeager, or too interested. He wanted to give Josephine the impression that he remained unimpressed, but still on the hook. He nodded his head slowly, encouraging her to continue.

"That's where Cooper comes in," Josephine continued. "Cooper takes a large portion of Eddy's monthly profit and, in exchange, he doesn't arrest him. Cooper takes bribe money from plenty of the city's bootleggers, but Eddy is Cooper's biggest profit-maker. If Eddy couldn't pay him, Cooper would be sunk. Oh, he'd be livid."

"Interesting," Patrick said. "How'd Edward get involved in the bootlegging industry in the first place? He worked with my cousin as a logger. How'd he get the money upfront to buy his liquor stills, transportation, bribe money?"

Josephine frowned and sipped her drink, looking up at the basement ceiling.

"You know," she said, "I hadn't really thought about that. I don't know, but I can keep my ears open if you'd like."

"That would be lovely," Patrick said. "I'd love to talk to him about it personally. But I don't want to get myself into trouble with an up-and-coming bootlegger. Or the police chief, for that matter."

Josephine smiled, eyeing Patrick. She felt a familiar sensation of mischief.

"I'm not sure what you're up to, Patrick Sullivan," Josephine, "and I don't want to know."

She looked around the room cautiously again. Her date was in the corner by the bar talking with the bartender and another gentleman.

"My date over there works accounts for Edward," Josephine said. "I overheard him talking about a party at Price Mansion next week. Henry Price, Jr. is trying to use his inheritance to jump into politics, so he's hosting a real high-class banquet to gather support from influential people. Naturally, Edward and Cooper will be there, and I guarantee they'll be talking business."

She paused and tapped her stemmed glass with her large pinky ring.

"And I think I can get you in," she said.

"I thought you might be able to finagle something," Patrick said. "What did you have in mind?"

"Well, we're in Cooper's basement," Josephine said. "His office is behind that curtain. I come here so often that no one would suspect anything if I went back there and looked around."

Josephine slid through the crowd, looking back at Patrick with a wink. She disappeared into the shadows, gracefully slipping through the curtain.

Patrick watched as Josephine's date spoke with Michael at the bar. Michael glanced slyly at Patrick, who gave him a glance that said *stall him*. So, Michael did. He spoke robustly about politics. He asked the man questions about his job, his favorite drinks, and his favorite speakeasies around the area. The man didn't even notice Josephine's disappearance, or her return.

Josephine emerged stealthily from behind the curtain and stood casually by Patrick. As she took a puff from her cigarette, she pulled two tickets from her left glove and passed them to Patrick. Placing them in his coat pocket, he smiled adoringly.

"Tickets to next week's party at Price Mansion," Josephine said. "They don't have Cooper's name on them, so you should be in the clear."

"You've still got it," Patrick said.

"Well, I ran around in your neighborhood long enough," Josephine said. "Those pickpocket skills don't just evaporate."

She winked at Patrick, who blushed in return.

"And don't worry," Josephine said. "There's nothing between me and the accountant. He's just paying for my drinks. You know I only have eyes for you, dear."

She kissed Patrick on the cheek. Looking at her empty drink glass, she waved to Patrick and disappeared into the crowd. Patrick caught Michael's attention and motioned his head toward the exit. Michael nodded to the bartender and met Patrick by the wooden staircase.

"Time to go," Patrick said.

They climbed the creaky stairs and emerged into the alleyway. Brisk air forced Michael to flip his coat collar up again. He looked at Patrick impatiently, waiting for him to give a detailed account of his conversation, which seemed crucial. Patrick glared. They needed more distance from the speakeasy before he could reveal his findings.

As the cousins turned onto 40th Avenue, they saw light rain glimmer in the streetlights. Crossing Hawthorne, Patrick thought they had walked far enough. He reached into his coat pocket and handed the tickets to Michael.

"Cousin," Patrick said, "are you ready to mingle with high society?"

Chapter 19

The key fit perfectly into the lock, just as Michael had hoped. He turned the knob and walked up the stairs to the loft. A small bed rested against the brick wall in the corner of the wide-open room. Two small windows looked out over the Willamette River; the Broadway Bridge's red cage was clearly visible.

"How'd you afford to buy this flat again?" Patrick asked.

"It's a long story," Michael said. "But a good friend left me some money."

"And you chose to buy a tiny loft?" Patrick said.

Michael laughed as he looked around the flat, admiring its simplicity.

"That same old friend also taught me about simplicity," Michael said. "Bringing material riches into your life invites trouble."

"Yeah, well I also heard that money buys happiness," Patrick said.

He paused and looked intently at the ceiling, placing his finger on his chin to indicate a serious contemplation.

"Maybe we could use your fat inheritance to buy our own stills and set up a speakeasy," Patrick continued. "We could be the next Rockefeller family."

Michael shook his head and laughed at his cousin.

"I'm only half-joking," Patrick said.

"I know," Michael said. "That's what makes it so amusing."

Michael reached into his duffel bag and removed Mr. Lao's leatherbound book. Closing the bag, he tossed it on the bed and placed the book on the table by the window. Streaks of sunlight filtered in through the window, illuminating dust particles in the still air inside the flat.

"What's with the book?" Patrick asked.

"It's leatherbound wisdom, cousin," Michael said. "I inherited it from Mr. Lao just before I left Shanghai. He taught me everything in it while I lived there. I still read it every day. It keeps me focused, grounded, balanced."

Patrick laughed, throwing his head back hyperbolically.

"Come on, cousin," Patrick said. "You know you can't read."

Michael shook his head and smiled, moving closer to the window to inspect the view. Patrick turned on the kitchen sink and filled a cup with water. He looked around the room and nodded approvingly.

"It's a small place," Patrick said. "If your friend, Mr. Lao, was as rich as you claim, it seems like you could have afforded something a little bigger. Maybe something with one of those crystal chandeliers."

He smiled facetiously as he opened each drawer in the kitchen.

"That's not my style," Michael said. "And besides, I promised Mr. Lao that I would use his money ethically. I don't need anything extravagant. This is only temporary until our plan plays out."

"Right, cousin," Patrick said. "Let's nail down this plot of ours."

He sat across from Michael at the wooden table and leaned forward on his elbows. The table wobbled slightly with the shift in weight. Sun beams shot through the window and illuminated the uneven floorboards, still coated in dust from vacancy.

The Sullivan cousins knew that Price's party was politically focused with the goal of raising funds for his campaign. This meant that some of the city's wealthiest, most notable people would attend. Aristocrats from old Portland families who wanted to maintain their reputation. Up-and-coming, debonair entrepreneurs, trying to gain a foothold in the city's influential circles. Anybody who wanted to have their family name mentioned in the daily papers.

"We know Edward will be there," Patrick said. "Josephine said that Cooper will be there, which makes sense. He is the police chief, after all."

"I bet the Stewarts will be there as well," Michael said. "Price will want to secure his influence, seeing as he has his hand in just about everything going on in the city, from hotels to water fountains."

"Mayor Baker might be in attendance," Patrick said. "Unless he sees Price as a political rival."

Michael nodded. He stood from his wooden chair and paced around the room, finally stopping to look out the window. The sun glistened off the Willamette River. A large ship moved away from the port. A train chugged along the tracks across the river toward Union Station.

"With all these high-powered people in the room, we can't just walk in as ourselves," Michael said. "All of these people run in the same circles. We need a backstory. Something believable. Something that makes us fit in with high society."

"You're right, cousin," Patrick said. "No one will recognize you. Everyone thinks you're dead. Plus, you shaved off your beard; I hardly recognize you myself. And no one will recognize me. I run with a different sort of crowd."

Michael returned his attention to the view from the window. The ship had swung parallel to the shore. Michael saw the ship's name; it was written in Chinese characters.

"So, what's our angle?" Patrick asked.

"I've got an idea," Michael said. "Do you know a tailor?"

* * *

The tailor stretched his measuring tape across Michael's shoulders and made chalk lines on the jacket. Patrick sat in a chair, nodding with superiority. Michael resisted the urge to laugh at his cousin.

After Michael and Patrick were fitted for their formal attire, Michael paid the tailor. They took their suits and walked across the Broadway Bridge toward Michael's new flat.

"Who'd have thought?" Michael said. "Two Irish lads from the East Side getting fitted for suits to rub elbows with the city's elite."

"Well, you came back from the dead," Patrick said. "So, I suppose anything is possible."

Yet something chipped away at Michael's thoughts. He climbed the stairs to the flat, furrowing his brow, trying to figure out a way around the obstacle.

"What's wrong, cousin?" Patrick asked as Michael opened the door.

"You and I," Michael said. "We were brought up a certain way. We learned certain manners and ways of interacting with

142

people. And those ways of interacting are much different than the rich folks that'll be at that party. When I was in Shanghai, I had to learn entirely new customs, mannerisms, and ways of doing things. Just because I wore local clothes and spoke Chinese didn't automatically make me fit in."

"What's your point, cousin?" Patrick asked.

"Just because we put on a couple of tuxedos doesn't mean we'll be able to fit in at Price Mansion," Michael said.

Patrick hung his suit in the closet and flopped on the bed.

"That's an easy one," Patrick said. "We just need to find someone to teach us how to act rich."

"Who do you have in mind?" Michael asked.

* * *

Josephine looked over her shoulder to make sure she wasn't followed. The sun rose over the river. Brisk air filled her lungs. A stark difference from the usual smoke-filled bars that she spent most of her time in. When Patrick phoned her and told her that Michael had returned, she couldn't believe it. She had to see him in person. And when Patrick told her about Edward's betrayal, she felt compelled to help.

She climbed the wooden steps and walked into Michael's flat. Patrick leaned against the brick wall, trying to hide his excitement.

"Hey, gents," she said. "Thanks for the call."

"Thank you for coming," Michael said. "Patrick here said you've made a business out of rubbing elbows with rich folks, so we figured you'd be the perfect person to teach us how to fit in."

"First I get you the tickets," Josephine said, "and now you

need my help again. You owe me."

Josephine half-smirked as she moved toward the window.

"We'll get you anything you need," Patrick said.

"Just keep me on your side when you take down these clowns," Josephine said. "I'm sick of the way they treat people, especially women. They stomp all over anybody who doesn't contribute directly to their rise to power. And they just look at me like some insignificant damsel with no power of my own. I'm just sick of it."

She hung her coat on the back of a chair and stood abruptly in front of the Sullivan cousins. Her down-to-business posture made Patrick stand tall.

"So, where do we start?" Josephine asked.

Michael opened a drawer that contained a minimal amount of silverware. He set the silverware on the table next to a plate and glass, motioning his hand toward the pile.

"How do we eat at a fancy dinner?" Michael asked.

Josephine rolled her eyes and walked over to the table. She arranged the plate, silverware, and glass according to their traditional high-society locations.

"Do you have another glass?" she asked.

Michael brought another glass to the table and Josephine placed it near the top of the arrangement.

"Now," Josephine said, "sit down."

Michael sat at the table, hunching his back forward to lean on his elbows. Josephine slapped his elbows away and forcibly straightened his posture.

"You can't sink into your seat like that, dear," Josephine said. "When you're at this party, you have to maintain a straight posture at all times. Don't let any of your weight fall onto the table."

"But it's so much more comfortable," Michael said.

"These wealthy families don't concern themselves with comfort," Josephine said. "They're concerned about appearances."

Josephine pointed to the fork on the outside of the place setting.

"Start from the outside and work your way in," she said. "And when the server comes to your spot, allow them to bend to your level before reaching for the serving utensil."

"That seems rude," Michael said.

"It very well does," Josephine said, "but that's what you have to do if you want to blend in."

Patrick laughed as he leaned against the brick wall, observing the situation. Josephine looked at Patrick with amusement.

"Don't think you're getting out of this either," Josephine said.

Michael returned the laugh to his cousin.

Gripping his fork, Michael pretended to eat. Josephine maneuvered his hand so he grasped the fork in a sophisticated manner. Michael worried he would drop the fork if he held it daintily, but he tried.

"Now drink," Josephine said.

Clutching his cup forcefully, he chugged water from his glass. Josephine snickered and adjusted his hand, forcing his pinky to stick out slightly. Michael rolled his eyes and sipped water slowly, eyeing Josephine's critique.

"During dinner, there will be superfluous conversation about topics that don't really matter much," Josephine said. "But it's imperative that you have an opinion if asked. So, study up. Go out and grab today's paper. And do the same every day until the night of the party."

She intensified her glare to Michael just to make sure he understood the gravity of the situation.

"You have to present yourself as an educated member of high society," Josephine continued. "And these folks always have an opinion about current events. Usually, their opinions favor the rich and look down on working-class people like us. Don't fall into the trap of voicing your *real* opinion. Remember, you're trying to blend in."

Patrick shrugged his shoulders and laughed.

"Easy enough," Patrick said. "What else do we need to worry about?"

Josephine smiled and walked over to Patrick. She wrapped her arm around his waist and clutched his hand.

"Dancing," Josephine said.

Patrick smirked.

"You don't have to worry about us," Patrick said. "The Sullivans are great dancers."

"But can you waltz?" Josephine said. "Foxtrot?"

Patrick's smile faded. He looked to Michael for support, but he had none to give.

"Well, not exactly," Patrick said. "But we can dance a mean jig."

"A jig will give you away immediately," Josephine said. "They'll pick out Irish jigs immediaitely, looking upon them as low-class. Portland's high society sticks with the traditional English dances. They're extremely boring, but again, if you want to blend in, it has to be done."

Michael sat in the windowsill and smirked as he watched Josephine drag Patrick around the room. She counted out each step in perfect rhythm, stopping her cadence occasionally to correct Patrick's steps.

The sun flickered off the river, drawing Michael's attention out the window and onto the street below. He noticed a figure standing across the street from the flat; the man had a distinctive scar on his cheek. He seemed out of place. Something about him signified high society, a projection which didn't fit in Michael's neighborhood. Maybe it was his cufflinks. Or maybe it was his perfectly pressed suit. The nerves in Michael's back twinged slightly. He tried to suppress the sense of fear.

"Alright, Mikey," Patrick said. "You're up."

Michael stood and practiced a dance with Josephine before she moved to the after-dinner process.

"It's customary at these types of events," Josephine said, "for the men to move into a smoking room and the ladies to move into another room for a while before the dancing begins. It gives the women time to gossip and the men time to smoke and talk business."

"Well, that seems boring," Michael said.

"I'm starting to get a sense that high society is actually very boring," Patrick added.

Josephine shook her head and threw her hands in the air.

"You two," she said. "This is perfect for you. This is your opportunity to talk with Cooper about Edward without the conversation seeming forced. It's expected to talk about business during this part of the party."

"You have a point," Patrick said.

Josephine reached into her purse and removed a bottle of whiskey. She held it up in the air; sunlight glistened through it.

"Where'd you get your hands on this?" Patrick asked.

"You know I can't tell you that," Josephine said.

She popped the cork from the bottle and poured a little whiskey into three glasses.

"Well, gents," she said. "You're as ready as you'll ever be."

"Thank you, darling," Patrick said.

Michael raised a glass and smiled. He watched Josephine and Patrick sip their whiskey, smitten with each other. Michael set his glass on the table, untouched. He glanced over his shoulder out the window. The scar-faced man was gone.

Chapter 20

The car trudged along the winding dirt road, straining to get up the hill. Michael adjusted his top hat; he wasn't used to wearing anything but a simple fedora or cap. And his necktie constricted his airways. He wasn't sure how to sit properly with tails on his tuxedo, either.

Patrick laughed from the other side of the carriage. Luckily for Patrick, he just had to wear a servant suit. No one would pay enough attention to him to notice if something was out of place.

"You should try to look even more uncomfortable," Patrick said.

"Knock it off," Michael said. "I've never worn fancy clothes like these before."

"Neither have I," Patrick said. "Except for that one time I stole a monocle and a pocket watch from a broker downtown. That was fun."

Michael shook his head and looked out the window. Lights from Price Mansion beamed through the forest in the West Hills.

"Now, you're sure you know Chinese?" Patrick asked.

"I spent three years over there," Michael said. "Of course I do."

"Just making sure," Patrick said. "If you're supposed to be the United States Ambassador to China tonight, you'd better be able to speak it. I don't want our cover getting blown because someone tests your skills."

"Well, since you're masquerading as my servant," Michael said, "I don't want our cover getting blown because you don't refer to me as *sir*."

Patrick smirked and waved him off.

"How about I refer to you as *Royal Bastard*," Patrick said.

Michael laughed, covering his laughter so the driver wouldn't hear it.

The car's engine revved up the damp dirt road and rounded the corner, revealing the glorious mansion. Its well-lit exterior accentuated the stone pillars, grandiose windows, and exquisite landscaping. The mansion was nestled atop a forested hill, hiding away from the commoners that worked downtown, all while preserving its pristine view of the city.

The car stopped underneath the mansion's stone overhang. Michael waved to his cousin, who snapped into character. Patrick jumped out of the carriage and held the door for Michael, who handed his top hat to his cousin before exiting in a dignified manner, just as he had practiced the last few days.

Other arriving guests watched Michael as he stood elegantly by the car's exterior. Catching Patrick's eye subtly, Michael snapped his fingers. Patrick gave Michael's top hat back to him, along with a cane. Patrick walked two steps behind Michael and they strolled to the entrance.

A man in a servant suit tipped his hat toward Michael. Michael handed his tickets to the servant, who took them and placed them in a basket. Then, taking his list from the table, he looked at Michael.

"And who may I have the pleasure of introducing?" the servant asked.

Patrick lifted his head toward the servant.

"The United States Ambassador to China," Patrick said. "Mr. Wilson."

The servant scanned his list with a pen. He flipped the page, and, with a confused expression, returned to the first page of the list.

"I'm embarrassed to say, sir," the servant said, "that we don't have your name on the list."

"Well, that's quite alright," Michael said. "It was a last-minute invitation. I've only just arrived from China."

"You do have tickets, though," the servant said. "So, no problem. Right in this way."

Michael tipped his hat to the servant. As he passed, he turned his head slightly to Patrick and winked. Patrick resisted the urge to laugh and tilted his head toward the steps.

As he walked into the mansion, his gaze lifted upward. Ornate windows, gaudy ironwork, and detailed wooden beams encompassed the room. Though it was two hours after sunset, the room felt remarkably well-lit.

The large crowd reflected off the massive windows in the ballroom. Patrick took Michael's coat and turned the corner to the coat check area. As he stepped through the crowd, he saw Edward. Patrick lowered his head toward his cousin, pretending to erase a scuff on his coat. As Edward passed, Patrick turned his head, hoping to catch Michael's attention.

But there was no need; Michael had seen Edward walking toward him. This was it. If Edward recognized Michael, the plan was over.

Edward walked suavely through the crowd. He nodded at

an acquaintance, continuing on his path. Michael stood firmly in place, tipping his top hat downwards to partially block his face.

As Edward moved in his direction, Michael held his ground. Without changing his path, Edward bumped into Michael, obviously expecting him to move out of his way. Looking up, Edward caught Michael's eye.

"Excuse me," Edward said. "It's customary to move out of the way when someone is walking in their direction."

Michael's heartbeat doubled. The nerves in his hands began to pulse.

"It might help to lift your eyes and watch where you're walking," Michael said.

Edward smiled and attempted to hide the anger in his eyes.

"Who do I have the pleasure of speaking with?" Edward asked.

Michael felt his breathing slow. His pulse calmed and his shoulders relaxed. Edward didn't recognize him.

"Wilson," Michael said. "U.S. Ambassador to China."

Edward's posture straightened instantly. His face contorted to feign humility.

"It's an honor to have you in our city, sir," Edward said. "Edward Bishop."

"Pleasure to meet you, Mr. Bishop," Michael said. "And what do you do that has earned you the distinction of being invited to such an illustrious event?"

Edward's eyes shifted.

"I'm a major force in our city's economy," Edward said.

"And I'm sure your city appreciates your sincere dedication to its economic growth," Michael said. "In fact, that's what more of our cities need. More honest, ethical businessmen like you."

Edward shifted his feet. He waved to someone in the crowd and tipped his hat to Michael.

"Ambassador," Edward said, "it has been an honor to make your acquaintance, but I must leave you. I do hope we get to discuss business later this evening."

Michael nodded approvingly. Edward hadn't recognized him. He was barely able to compose his excitement.

As Edward disappeared into the crowd, Michael turned to find Patrick sampling the food platters that lined the wall. He looked approvingly at Patrick and wiped the sweat from his brow. Michael stood next to Patrick, but faced away from him toward the crowd.

"How's the food?" Michael asked.

"Real good," Patrick said. "The shrimp is cold."

"He didn't recognize me," Michael said. "And he bought my cover identity."

"That's great news, cousin," Patrick said. "Without that scruffy, Irish bear, you do look halfway respectable."

Michael saw the crowd part. A bearded man swaggered through the crowd and opened his arms wide as he walked toward Michael. Looking from side to side, Michael couldn't determine the man's focus point. As he neared Michael, the stranger embraced him. Michael looked to Patrick for help, but the gazing crowd inhibited any drastic moves.

"Ambassador," the man said. "I'm so pleased you were able to make it to the party."

"Well," Michael said, "I'm just happy I could make it."

Patrick shifted his eyes back and forth toward a portrait on the wall that depicted Henry Price, Jr., a spitting image of the man who has just embraced him.

"Mr. Price," Michael said, "how is the campaign going?"

"It's going well, Ambassador," Price said. "And after tonight's turnout, I have no doubt that my momentum will continue into office. And with a man of your position at this function, my reputation can only increase."

Another man approached the conversation. Price stepped to the side, inviting him into the discussion.

"Ambassador," Price said, "let me introduce Gregory Stewart. He's one of the city's finest philanthropists."

Michael shook Stewart's hand. The thought of Stewart's water fountains in the center of the city struck Michael as ironic. Stewart had installed running water fountains throughout the city to deter men from drinking alcohol. Now, he was conducting political business with a major bootlegger and a man who had made a business through the Shanghai Tunnels.

At least Stewart's *heart was in the right place*, Michael thought.

"It's a pleasure to meet you, Mr. Stewart," Michael said.

"How are things in China these days, Ambassador?" Stewart asked.

Michael froze temporarily. He had spent the last three years in China, but his understanding of China's place in global politics and its relationship with the United States was minimal. And a man with Stewart's business interests would be fully aware of the situation. Michael hadn't thought this part of the plan through.

"Overall, things are going well," Michael said. "The warlords have been kept relatively at arm's length, allowing our business interests to expand, especially into Shanghai."

Stewart nodded in agreement. Michael fished his memory, searching for more accurate pieces of information to keep the conversation flowing. Luckily, another man approached the group.

"Pardon me gentlemen," Price said, "but I must introduce the Ambassador to another prominent member of our community. May I present Franklin Cooper, Portland's Chief of Police."

Michael shook hands with Cooper, who then shook hands with Stewart in a more casual manner. His formal police suit struck Michael as excessive.

"I had the damnedest time getting in," Cooper said. "I couldn't find my tickets anywhere. I swear I'm getting older by the minute."

Michael laughed audibly, encouraging Stewart and Price to do the same, albeit for different reasons unknown to them.

"Gentlemen," Price said, "I must excuse myself. I have an old friend that just walked in."

Price tipped his hat and excused himself from the conversation, moving to another group of influential people. Potential donors, most likely.

"Well, Chief Cooper," Stewart said. "I want to commend you on your efforts in keeping the deadly scourge of alcohol off of our streets."

Michael choked on his water, resisting the urge to laugh and spit his water back into his cup. Stewart looked at Michael with temporary concern before returning his attention back to Cooper.

"I see your efforts almost daily in Price's newspapers," Stewart continued.

"We're just doing our job to keep our city safe," Cooper said. "It's because of donations and initiatives like your fountains that we're able to be so successful."

As Michael listened to Cooper speak, he saw Edward move

through the crowd with purpose in his eyes. He stood near the corner of the ballroom suspiciously. A familiar-looking man with a scar on his face approached, nodded at Edward, and moved into an empty, unlit drawing room. Edward followed.

Michael knew he had to be in that room to hear the conversation. He excused himself from Stewart and Cooper and casually poured some tea in a cup near the drawing room entrance. Nodding at Patrick, Michael moved efficiently and discreetly through the crowd. He leaned against a beam and sipped his tea. His ear leaned into the drawing room, where he heard Edward's distinctive voice begin to speak.

"I can make you a very powerful man," Edward said. "Are you ready to hear the plan?"

Chapter 21

Lights from the ballroom flickered as they reflected into the drawing room. Dusty bookshelves lined the shadowed walls. Edward stood in the corner next to the man with the scar on his face. He leaned on his cane arrogantly, scanning the room to make sure no one else was privy to the conversation.

Michael stood just around the corner outside the room, but he could see through the space between the door hinges. Edward's voice channeled directly into his ear.

"I'll make my run for Mayor next year," Edward said. "And I want you to be my right-hand man."

Adjusting the angle of his ear, Michael learned further into the doorway.

"Given your time with the police department and your skills in security," Edward said, "I'll make you my new police chief. We'll take over the whole town. We'll create laws that make our operation even more efficient and covert than it already is."

"I like the sound of that," the scar-faced man said. "But what about Cooper?"

Michael sensed a long pause; he assumed Edward was smirking.

"That's the tricky part," Edward said. "Cooper continues to raise our rates because he has all the negotiating power. We need to get him out of office, but he'll definitely tell the papers everything about our operation if we let him go."

"You want me to off him?" the scar-faced man said.

"Once I win the race for Mayor," Edward said.

Michael's eyes widened. He scanned the ballroom, watching as Cooper continued to speak with Stewart and a growing crowd of influential city elite.

"What makes you so confident that you'll win?" the scar-faced man asked.

"I have deeper pockets," Edward said. "We can campaign, buy votes, and bribe officials to guarantee us the Mayor's office."

"And your past won't..." the scar-face man started.

Edward paused, drawing his pride toward the bookshelf.

"Any information on Josephine?" Edward asked. "I've had you following her for a while now. You have to have something useful by now."

The scar-faced man's breathing quickened. He stammered a bit, nervous to disappoint Edward's powerful presence.

"Nothing significant," the scar-faced man said. "I tracked her to an apartment building in a rough neighborhood in North Portland last week, hoping she would lead me to him, but I got nothing."

"And she doesn't suspect you tailing her?" Edward asked.

"Not that I can tell," the scar-faced man said.

He paused, reading Edward's body language. Determining his approval, he continued.

"What happens if I find him?" the scar-faced man asked.

Edward ran a comb through his greased hair and looked out the window. His hollow reflection looked back at him.

The long silence worried Michael. He turned his head to look through the crack in the door. His eyes met the scar-faced man's gaze as he looked toward the doorway. Michael's heart began to race again; he pulled away from the door and flattened himself against the wall.

Quick footsteps echoed from the drawing room. Michael breathed deeply, calming his pulse. Swiftly, he disappeared into the crowd, where he started a casual conversation with someone about the view of the city from the house.

Peripherally, Michael saw the scar-faced man stand at the drawing room entrance. Above his scar, his heavy eyes scanned the area, looking for anyone who could have heard the conversation. As the man moved from the drawing room, Edward walked out and moved in the other direction. Michael saw Edward disappear into another room.

Looking over his shoulder, Michael evaporated into the crowd. He put more focus on the scar-faced man's vision than his own path. And then his shoulder bumped into someone.

"Excuse me," a female voice shouted.

Michael whipped his head around and saw the most beautiful woman in the world looking back at him.

Emma, Michael thought.

She looked at Michael, intent on receiving an apology. Michael searched her eyes for any trace of recognition. There was none.

"I'm terribly sorry, miss," Michael said. "I wasn't watching where I was going."

"That's obvious enough," Emma said.

Michael looked around quickly for Edward. He didn't see Edward anywhere; however, he did catch Patrick's attention. Patrick stood in the corner of the room shaking his head vehemently. He pointed his finger toward the door, trying to tell Michael to leave Emma alone for now. Ignoring his cousin, Michael deviated from the plan.

"Can I redeem myself with a dance?" Michael asked.

Emma raised her eyebrows, unsure of how to respond. She scanned the crowd for Edward.

"Well, I suppose one dance couldn't do anything more to damage your actions," Emma said.

Taking Emma's hand, Michael led her to the dance floor, where slow, classical music wafted from the band on a small stage. Just as Michael had practiced, he led Emma in a boring, rigid, classical dance, the pinnacle of high society.

"And who do I have the pleasure of dancing with?" Michael asked.

"Emma," she said. "And who might you be?"

"Wilson," Michael said. "United States Ambassador to China."

"What an honor," Emma said facetiously.

Michael laughed. Even though she was now a member of high society, Emma's contempt for snobbery still captivated him.

"And you, Ms. Emma," Michael said. "You must be the Princess of Wales?"

"I certainly am," she said.

They both laughed playfully. Michael looked into her eyes and she returned the gaze. Michael couldn't help but feel the chemistry, the friction, the connection. It felt as though he had never left.

Her hand felt warm and comfortable on his shoulder. Her hair was pinned up, but a few strands fell and brushed Michael's cheek. He felt himself begin to blush. He wasn't certain, but he thought he sensed her move closer to him, pressing herself against the ring that hung underneath his shirt; the ring that was meant for her.

As the music floated magically through the ballroom, Michael felt a forceful tap on his shoulder. He turned to see Edward standing in front of him; a stern expression engrossed his face. Emma looked frustrated; she was enjoying the dance.

"Excuse me, Ambassador, but I'm going to cut in," Edward said. "She's mine."

"I do apologize," Michael said with a hint of sarcasm.

He nodded to Emma and winked. Edward noticed the wink and abruptly stepped in front of Michael.

"Let me show you how a real gentleman dances with a lady," Edward said.

"Edward," Emma said, "that was rude."

She pushed him away.

"And another thing," Emma said, "I'm not *yours*. We just happen to be engaged, but I belong to no one but myself."

Edward snickered.

"You're such a progressive," Edward mocked. "I assume you'll want to vote in the next election with those other women who pretend to play politics?"

Michael stepped forward, putting his hands in front of him as if to block any more insults toward Emma.

"Hey, now," Michael said. "There's no need to treat anybody with such contempt. And I happen to love the fact that women finally have a say in their country. It's long overdue."

Edward broke from Emma and stood face-to-face with Michael. He glared into Michael's eyes. As he tilted his head, Michael senses a faint recognition begin to form in Edward's

161

mind.

Each man seemed to grow taller, arching their chins upward, daring the other to make a move. Rage pulse through Michael's veins. His heart thumped through his chest. But as he breathed purposefully, he was able to calm his emotions, control his rage.

Mr. Lao echoed in Michael's mind. *Be calm; you can only control your own actions. Balance will control the actions of others.*

Edward's neck twitched. His hands balled into fists. Michael waited for Edward to punch him, to attempt to tackle him to the ground. Michael knew what his first defensive maneuver would be, but he wanted to go on the attack. He wanted to knock Edward out in front of Emma, to expose him for the fraud that he was.

Again, Mr. Lao's voice echoed in Michael's memory, urging him to maintain his sense of balance, encouraging Michael to find his center.

Patrick emerged stealthily through the crowd. He tapped Michael on the shoulder and bowed his head to feign servitude.

"Excuse me, Ambassador," Patrick said, "but your presence has been requested in the lobby."

A sense of urgency rang in his voice. Michael returned his attention to Edward. A long silence gripped them. As Michael glared, he thought he saw Edward's pupils dilate, but only momentarily. He thought he sensed terror, but only momentarily.

Then, intentionally breaking his focus, Michael looked at Emma. He smiled kindly, a sentiment which she returned. Michael tipped his hat, turned, and followed Patrick through the crowd.

When they entered the lobby, Michael stopped. Patrick nudged Michael to keep moving. It was time to leave.

"What were you thinking?" Patrick whispered as they walked to the car.

"I couldn't help myself," Michael said.

Patrick rolled his eyes and opened the car door.

"I thought you were supposed to be the calm one," Patrick said.

Chapter 22

The dim lights reflected off of the red leather in the back room of the Bald Eagle as Michael sat in his usual booth. A musician wailed on his saxophone over a jazzy drummer. Another musician walked his fingers down the bass.

The adrenaline from the evening's encounter with Edward had almost worn off, but revenge still occupied every section of Michael's thoughts. And the love he still felt from Emma created a newfound sense of urgency. And jealousy.

Patrick returned from the bar with two glasses of Irish whiskey and sat across from Michael. He raised his glass. Michael did the same. Sipping his whiskey slowly, he let the saxophone fill the silence until Patrick couldn't handle it anymore.

"Aside from your hatred for Edward," Patrick said, "what did we find out tonight?"

Michael smirked, shaking his head at his cousin's remark.

"The conversation I overheard in the drawing room might come into play," Michael said.

"Interesting, cousin," Patrick said. "What did you overhear?"

Michael leaned forward and lowered his voice.

"We know that Eddy wants to run for Mayor," Michael said.

"Once he becomes Mayor, he'll remove Cooper from his role as Police Chief."

"If Eddy pushes Cooper out, he won't have to pay him bribe money anymore," Patrick said.

"Exactly," Michael said. "How do you think Cooper is going to react?"

Patrick's eyes widened. He shook his head violently, taking another sip of whiskey to calm his sentiments.

"Cooper is going to kill him," Patrick said. "Or worse. Think about how much information Cooper has on Eddy. He could rat him out to the Feds. Cooper could even make a play like he was plotting it the whole time."

Michael leaned in closer to Patrick and lowered his voice.

"I overheard Eddy say he's going to kill Cooper once he wins the Mayor race," Michael said.

"Makes sense," Patrick said. "It's Eddy's only way to keep Cooper quiet."

Patrick looked at his glass and noticed that it was empty. He stood, nodded to Michael, and walked to the bar. The bartender poured more whiskey into Patrick's glass before returning to his post, where he listened to the saxophone player riff over a slick drum beat. Patrick returned to the booth with a distinct smile on his face.

"I've got it," Patrick said.

"Got what, cousin?" Michael asked.

"Cooper is our man," Patrick said. "He has everything to lose if Eddy becomes Mayor, and everything to gain if he doesn't. Therefore, Cooper will want to act on any information we give him about this situation. A situation about which he is unaware."

Michael laughed at his cousin's intentional pretentiousness.

"And, let's face it," Patrick said. "Once Eddy becomes Mayor, Emma is locked into marriage. She'd be a fool to leave the Mayor."

Michael dropped his head onto the table. It thudded against the dense wood. He groaned and slowly lifted his eyes.

"Sorry, cousin," Patrick said.

"Don't be sorry," Michael said. "You're absolutely right."

Couples danced to the up-tempo jazz music that fluttered from the corner of the room. They danced so happily. It made Michael sick to think that he could have been out there with Emma. She would have been his wife by now. He would have been her husband. They would have lived somewhere outside the city. Probably on a small farm with a fence. A tall pine tree shading the front porch. A few children running around the yard.

But Edward took that opportunity from him. Selfishness and greed prevailed, turning friendship into betrayal.

Michael wanted Edward dead. And he wanted to do it himself.

Mr. Lao whispered to Michael. A sense of guilt twisted Michael's stomach. He knew vengeance wasn't the ethical response.

But maybe vengeance was justice.

"We have to do something about Eddy," Michael said. "I don't want to kill him. But we need to do something."

Patrick looked down at his whiskey. It swirled in his glass. Taking a sip, he placed his glass back down on the table and lifted his eyes to Michael.

"Let's Shanghai him."

* * *

Michael stood across the street from the city's police headquar-ters. The building looked ominous. Thick stones presented an impenetrable facade. Tall pillars produced prison-like shadows. Large iron doors gave the impression that the building was barricaded, fortified.

Leaning against a light post, Michael watched as two po-licemen left the building. They strolled down the sidewalk, smirking as they walked.

The sun peeked out from behind the clouds, creating a small rainbow in the mist before it returned to its hiding place. A shadow cast itself over the building again.

Michael's attention wandered up the building towering walls. Then, he snapped his focus back to the entrance. The door had opened. This time, it was Cooper.

Michael adjusted his petticoat. He flipped his collar up to conceal his face. He pulled the brim of his cap down to shadow his eyes. Calming his breathing and composure, he walked briskly to keep pace with Cooper, mirroring his movements from the opposite sidewalk.

Cooper turned down Ankeny Street toward the river, away from Michael. A car honked at Michael as he crossed the street, so he quickened his pace and hoped the chief hadn't seen him.

As Cooper approached the street corner, he stopped and leaned against a brick building. Michael slowed his speed and leaned against the building near Cooper. Without looking directly at the chief, he spoke in a low voice.

"Someone is out to get you," Michael said.

Cooper snapped his head toward Michael. His face began to turn red with anger.

"Who the hell are you?" Cooper asked.

"Someone with a mutual acquaintance," Michael said.

Shifting his eyes, Cooper struggled to determine Michael's angle.

"If you hurt me, you're a dead man," Cooper said. "I'm a cop. The whole force will be after you."

Michael laughed and sank casually into the wall. He needed Cooper to relax.

"I'm not here to hurt you," Michael said. "I'm here to save your life."

"Who sent you?" Cooper said.

"No one sent me," Michael said. "I'm just a concerned citizen looking out for our Police Chief."

Cooper tipped his hat upward and eyed Michael. A look of familiarity crossed his face, but Cooper couldn't quite pinpoint how he recognized Michael.

"Alright, wise guy," Cooper said. "Who's out to get me?"

Michael turned and looked directly into the chief's eyes.

"Edward Bishop," Michael said.

Cooper's eyebrows shot up, exposing the whites of his eyes. He looked around frantically, uncomposed. He stepped closer to Michael and grabbed his shoulder.

"We can't talk here," Cooper said. "Too many ears."

He pushed Michael into the brick building. Michael followed Cooper down an old wooden staircase. Cooper knocked on the iron door at the bottom of the corridor. A tall, well-dressed man opened it and ushered Cooper and Michael into the dark room.

"You're a little early today, sir," the well-dressed man said.

"Something came up," Cooper said. "You have a booth where this gentleman and I can talk?"

The well-dressed man waved his arm toward a booth near the back of the room. Michael's eyes began to adjust to the dim light. He saw a few barstools, wooden tables, and black leather booths lining the wall. The room was small, a perfect speakeasy size. Apparently, Cooper frequented this stop regularly. Or maybe he collected payments from the owner. Or maybe both.

"Now, tell me," Cooper said, "how did you come by this information that Bishop is out to get me? That's a bold accusation."

Michael smiled; he had successfully obtained Cooper's interest.

"I heard it with my own two ears," Michael said.

"Alright, then," Cooper said. "Tell me what you know."

"Eddy is planning to run for Mayor," Michael said. "When he wins, he's going to remove you as Police Chief. He doesn't want to pay you anymore, you see. He's getting greedy."

Cooper threw his head back and laughed.

"Bishop can't remove me from my post," Cooper said. "I know too much about him. I could ruin his political career before it even gets started."

Michael looked around and leaned in closer. He wanted his next statement to appear dramatic.

"And Eddy knows that, you see," Michael said. "That's why he's going to kill you."

Cooper leaned back in his seat and slapped his palm against his forehead. Sweat began to bead on his neck. Heat seemed to rise in the room.

"And why are you telling me this?" Cooper asked.

"We have a common enemy, Mr. Cooper," Michael said.

The well-dressed man brought two martinis to the table. He nodded subtly to Cooper, who returned the nod, indicating that everything was fine.

"Since you're telling me this information rather than keep it to yourself," Cooper said, "I presume you want me to act on it somehow."

"I do, sir," Michael said. "I need you to get rid of Edward Bishop."

Cooper shifted his eyes back and forth, weighing his options. He sipped his drink quickly, hoping to find some inspiration in the bottom of his gin concoction.

"I can't do it," Cooper said. "My position is high-profile. If I arrest Bishop, he'll ruin me. He would out me as a crooked cop. And I can't have him whacked; someone would trace it back to me and the Feds would take me down."

Michael leaned forward. Cooper's pause worried him.

"It has to be you," Cooper said. "I can set you up and I'll look the other way. I can make sure my boys do the same. But it has to be you."

"How can we send him to Shanghai?" Michael asked.

Cooper looked upward, as if racking his own brain. He tapped his nose and leaned forward.

"He brings me my cut personally once a month at Quimby's," Cooper said. "It would be a guaranteed stop for him that I could orchestrate without drawing any suspicion"

He gulped his martini and set his glass on the table. As he stood from his booth seat, he turned and faced Michael.

"But you'll have to orchestrate it from below," Cooper said. "It's up to you to go into the tunnels and arrange the drop. I can't be seen there, or else people will talk"

Cooper stood and tipped his cap to Michael. He nodded to the bartender, tossing him a coin to pay for the drinks.

As Cooper left the dark room, Michael felt his nerves fire. Fear gripped him. The thought of returning into the tunnels brought about his darkest shadows. His palms began to sweat.

His legs began to shake. His vision began to close.

"Hey, chap," the bartender said. "You alright?"

Michael concentrated on his breathing. Mr. Lao echoed in his memory.

His vision began to return and he regained control of his extremities. Looking at the bartender, he nodded somewhat convincingly.

Standing, Michael walked to the iron door and climbed the rickety wooden stairs. As he stepped on the street, he let the light rain calm him. Nature brought him back to balance.

But fear persisted, wrestling with balance for control.

Chapter 23

Michael stood alone at the entrance to the tunnels. The sun began to set; a light rain fell behind him, eclipsing the river in a shadowy mist. He dug his boots into the dirt that lined the river's edge. People laughed and moved purposefully above him, but all he could hear was the river, its flow echoed through the dark tunnel entrance.

He took a step forward and froze. His hands trembled with fear. His pulse quickened and his peripheral vision blurred. A groan reverberated from somewhere inside the tunnel, sending flashbacks of shackles, ships, and death through his mind.

Retreating two steps, he paused again. He had waited for revenge for three years. He had plotted, planned, and pleaded for retribution. But that vengeance would only come at his own willingness to conquer his fear.

Flipping his coat collar up to block the chill, he moved forward, entering the darkness of the Shanghai Tunnels.

His muddy footsteps reverberated off the stone walls. The sounds of chains and groans echoed through the tunnel, sending chills up Michael's back. His pupils began to widen as his eyes got used to the darkness. He could distinguish shadowy shapes moving through the interconnected passageways. Voices rang out somewhere in the network, barking orders at someone. Maybe a prisoner. Maybe a bootlegger. Maybe no one at all.

He remembered waking up on the dirt floor with a headache. He remembered the feeling of the chains that shackled him, the voices he heard around him, and the other prisoners who terrified him. He remembered the guard, the dens, and the promiscuous rooms. He remembered it all.

As he continued to walk deeper into the tunnels, he passed a red door. It seemed out of place against the rough stone and dirt walls. A woman leaned sensually against the stone, batting her eyes at Michael.

"Can I help you, honey?" the woman asked.

Michael's heart raced faster; his breathing became constricted, irregular.

"Uh, no thanks," Michael said.

Michael quickened his pace.

He slowed his stroll as he rounded the corner. He had left the light of the red door and returned to the shadows of the tunnels. He stepped slowly to let his eyes adjust, hesitant about what he would find.

Panic began to take control. He leaned against a dirt wall for support. Then, he heard the voice of Mr. Lao somewhere inside his memory, telling him to breath, to find balance.

As he continued through the tunnel, a familiar smell wafted through the air, a smell he hadn't experienced in nearly three years. Opium.

Another light appeared, dimly illuminating an open room. As Michael passed, he saw men laying in triple-level bunk beds, their eyes glossed over with a distinct haze. Some laughed uncontrollably. Others looked up at the ceiling with no trace of consciousness.

A mustached man in a vest popped out from around the corner. His eyes were alert, exploding with vice.

"You want to give it a try?" the man said. "We've got a bottom bunk open for you. A little more expensive, but you won't fall off."

Michael shook his head confidently and kept walking. The man continued to shout his sales pitch to Michael as he moved through the tunnels.

As he left the opium den's light, his pupils tried to adjust again. Walking in partial blindness, Michael noticed the smell of dampness, of dirt, of liquor and mold. Each step seemed to grow colder. And then he felt it. The crunch of glass underneath his boot.

He stopped and allowed his eyes to catch up to the darkness. Finally, he looked up, and there it was. A faint light outlined the trapdoor into Quimby's. The same trapdoor he fell through three years ago. The same trapdoor that altered the entire course of his life.

"You lost?" a gruff voice shouted from somewhere in the darkness.

Michael jumped. His arms shot out in front of him a defensive position, instinct born from three years of training.

A man emerged into the subtle light from the trapdoor. Michael analyzed his face. A distinctive scar cut across the man's cheek.

"I know who you are," Michael said. "You're Edward Bishop's man, aren't you?"

The man's eyes shifted from side to side.

"Who's asking?" the man said.

"That's not important," Michael said, attempting to bolster his confidence.

"And why not?" the man asked.

Michael reached into his pocket and removed a large stack of cash. He strategically placed it in front of the trapdoor's light.

"Because I have a proposition for you," Michael said.

Chapter 24

Light beamed into Michael's closed eyelids. A rare morning of late spring sunlight pierced through the thin curtain. He turned over in his bed and shoved his face into the pillow. The day's necessary task was already weighing on his mind.

He didn't have to do it, but it was the ethical move. He knew he should. Mr. Lao would have wanted this to happen. Honesty as opposed to revenge. Restoration as its own form of justice.

Michael placed his cap on his head and buttoned his simple vest. Opening the door, he stepped down the flight of stairs and onto the street. He had a long walk ahead of him. The river smelled fishy as he walked briskly along its edge.

The Hawthorne Bridge's counterweights towered above the river. As he approached, he felt his nerves begin to control him. He breathed deeply through his nose and exhaled through his mouth. He concentrated on simply being present. He concentrated on balance.

Stepping onto the bridge's walkway, he looked down through the steel-grated floor. The river's fast water rushed far below his feet. Michael stopped when he reached the bridge's center point. He looked over the edge, watching early morning row boats and small-scale shipping vessels move in and out of downtown ports. Some delivered supplies and food. He knew some were responsible for more illicit products.

The sunlight sparkled along the river, but clouds approached rapidly from the west.

Michael waited. Thirty minutes had passed. He knew they were coming. Patrick had gathered some information from a reliable source that they walked this way each Tuesday morning.

But maybe they wouldn't. Maybe Michael had been too careless in his pursuit. Checking his pocket watch, he decided to wait for another half hour. Michael rubbed the beard stubble that had grown on his face. He decided not to shave in hopes that it would bring about a sense of recognition.

And then he saw them. Walking toward him from the west side of the bridge, they looked small. Michael could sense tension brewing between them. The way they walked with each other appeared cold.

Michael's feet trembled. He couldn't decide if it was the steel-grated floor that shook with their steps, or if it was Emma's presence making his heart flutter, or if it was repressed hatred brewing from the sight of Edward.

"Lovely day, isn't it?" Michael said as Emma and Edward approached.

When Emma looked at Michael, her eyes softened. She looked at him longingly. Somehow, Michael sensed that she recognized him for who he truly was.

Edward, on the other hand, looked impatient.

"Mr. Ambassador," Edward said. "I thought you would have made your trip back to China by now."

Michael turned his feet and stood face-to-face with Edward.

He straightened his posture, throwing his shoulders back, lifting his chin. His pulse quickened, but his controlled breathing calmed his presence.

"Don't play innocent with me, Eddy," Michael said. "You know exactly who I am."

Edward shifted nervously. He caught his foot as it slipped on the damp steel grate. His eyes darted to Emma before returning to Michael's intense stare.

"Mr. Ambassador," Edward said. "I'm not entirely sure what you're referring to."

"Tell her, Eddy," Michael said.

Edward clutched Emma's shoulder and attempted to usher her away, to continue their walk. But Emma refused. She stood, firmly planted on the steel-grate walkway, looking emphatic, yet confident.

"Tell me what, Edward?" Emma said.

"Nothing, dear," Edward said. "I think the Ambassador is a bit confused."

Michael reached into his jacket pocket and removed the knife, flicking the blade open with precision. Before Edward could flinch, Michael had the blade pressed against Edward's throat. Michael grabbed Edward by the collar with his free hand and slammed him against the railing. The river raged below; Michael had complete control.

"Tell her the truth, Eddy," Michael shouted.

"You wouldn't," Edward said.

"You haven't seen me in three years," Michael shouted. "You have no idea what I've been through. You have no idea what I'm capable of!"

Emma lurched forward and grabbed Michael by the arm. She threw her entire momentum backward, trying to dislodge the knife. Michael didn't budge. Emma wept, she screamed and flailed.

"Tell her the truth!" Michael shouted again.

"This man is deranged, Emma!" Edward shouted.

Edward grinned nervously, the type of grin that accompanied guilt. As he grinned, Emma's grip on Michael's arm relaxed. She moved away from Edward and looked to Michael with a sense of acknowledgement. Then, her face presented total recognition. She didn't need an explanation from Edward; the entire story was written in Michael's face.

"She knows, Eddy," Michael said. "Maybe not every last detail, but she knows."

Edward laughed; the laugh echoed off the steel with desperation.

"That foolish girl doesn't know anything," Edward said. "She only plays at being intelligent."

Michael wanted to carve his knife into Edward's throat, but before he could move, Emma's palm connected directly with Edward's jaw. Michael smirked as he saw Emma's face flare.

"Alright, alright," Edward shouted. "I'll tell her. Just get that thing away from my neck."

Michael released the knife's pressure, but maintained a strong hold on his collar. Edward looked at Michael with contempt, though he appeared disheveled. Looking at the floor beneath Emma, Edward began to speak.

"This is Michael Sullivan," Edward said.

Emma began to weep. She nervously touched Michael's arms, his face. Then, she recoiled.

"How?" Emma asked. "How, Edward?"

"Three years ago, I was in a low place," Edward said. "I wanted Michael's life. He had it all: goals, morals, a suitable wife, and the ability to rise in financial status. I wanted his life. I wanted to regain my family's good name."

Emma looked at Edward with pure hatred.

"What did you do to him?" Emma asked.

Edward tried to walk toward her, but Michael strengthened his grip on the collar, freezing Edward in his place.

"I reached out to one of my family's old associates," Edward said. "He found a way for me to make a large profit at the expense of Michael's disappearance, which would allow me to step into his life. So, I had him Shanghaied."

Michael pushed Edward away. Edward staggered backward, smacking his head on a steel beam. He looked at Michael with stern, unwavering eyes. He couldn't look at Emma.

"Eddy," Michael said. "You were my best friend. You were like a brother to me."

Edward opened his mouth to speak, but Michael held up his hand with a sense of command that made Edward pause.

"I forgive you," Michael said.

Raising his eyes in astonishment, Edward looked at Michael with disbelief.

"Honestly, Eddy, I forgive you," Michael said. "But there are others who might not be so forgiving. You need to leave Portland tonight and never return."

Edward raised an eyebrow at Michael. He seemed unconvinced.

"Consider this your warning," Michael said. "I have forgiven you. I have made peace with what you have done. And, as part of your own penance, you need to take accountability for your actions and leave town. Start over somewhere else."

"And if I stay?" Edward asked.

"Your whole life will change," Michael said. "I know that

from experience."

Michael backed away from Edward, giving him space to make a decision.

"Emma," Edward said, "come with me."

Wiping a tear from her eye, Emma reached toward her own hand. She removed Edward's engagement ring and threw it at him. The ring hit Edward in the nose before dropping to the steel-grate floor. Its bounce echoed in silence as it fell through the grate. Splashing in the river, it was washed away.

Emma shook her head, wiped her face, and fled across the bridge the same way she had arrived. Her footsteps shook the floor. As the sound of her steps faded, Edward laughed and looked at Michael with conviction.

"You made a big mistake by coming back to Portland, Sully," Edward said.

He continued to face Michael as he backed away across the bridge. His eerie laugh reflected off the steel beams. As he faded away, he shouted again.

"And you made an even bigger mistake by not killing me when you had the chance," Edward shouted.

A fog rolled across the river, engulfing the bridge.

"You'll pay for this, Sully!"

Chapter 25

A shadow concealed the corner booth at Quimby's where Patrick sat. He sipped on whiskey to calm his nerves. The bartender had poured him a glass after Patrick used the proper code word, a trick he had heard about from an old accomplice of his. He checked his pocket watch for the fifth time in a minute, routinely watching the door.

He's late, Patrick thought.

Patrick had gathered some information about Quimby's. He found out which night Edward made his bribe drop-off to Cooper. Sometimes, the bootlegger and the cop would discuss business in coded language in order to conceal their information. The meetings were prompt, but efficient, Patrick's informant said. And Edward was never late.

As he took another drink, he saw a light reflect onto the ceiling; the door had opened. Patrick's eyes darted upward to see his cousin glide into the bar. Without making eye contact with the bartender, Michael moved to the corner booth and sat with his cousin in the shadows.

"You had me worried, cousin," Patrick said, his voice low. "You were supposed to be here at 7:15. It's almost 7:30."

"Did you think I got captured by his goons or something?" Michael said.

Patrick nodded and took another drink.

"You need a drink to calm your nerves?" Patrick asked.

"No thanks," Michael said. "I don't need that stuff. I want to keep my mind clear."

"Whatever you say, pious one," Patrick said.

Michael smiled and shook his head as Patrick took another drink.

They waited in near-silence, attempting to blend in, attempting to melt into the shadows. And, at this hour of the night, that was easy enough to do. Most of the tables were full of restaurant patrons. Most drank water, but the few who knew the code word drank whiskey concoctions. Some likely snuck in their own spirits. Loud and boisterous tables drew attention away from Michael and Patrick's shadowy corner booth.

"I can't believe you confronted the bastard," Patrick said. "You should have just let him meet his fate."

"It wouldn't have been right," Michael said. "I couldn't stoop to his level. I had to give him a chance at redemption."

"How'd a guy like you get so noble?" Patrick said, smirking.

Michael laughed and waved off his cousin.

"You think he's going to show up?" Patrick asked.

"I hope not," Michael said.

"He wouldn't be stupid enough to show up after your warning," Patrick said. "Would he?"

Michael shook his head. As much as he wanted revenge, he wanted to see Edward move forward through redemption even more. He knew that balance would be restored somehow. He had done his part to set the plan in motion. It was up to Edward to determine the outcome.

"7:55," Patrick said, checking his watch again.

Michael watched the door underneath his low-brimmed cap.

The door opened and Chief Cooper entered, dressed in plain clothes. He sat at the bar and nodded to the bartender, who poured a drink and handed it to Cooper discreetly. As Cooper lifted his glass to take a drink, he looked into the shadows of the corner booth, nodding in acknowledgment. Patrick raised his glass slightly above the table in return.

"Cooper is ready," Michael said. "I'll bet he's hoping Eddy shows up so he can take him down. Not that I'm a fan of Cooper's ethics, but he's the lesser of two evils."

"Oh, Cooper looks ready, alright," Patrick said.

Cooper took a swing of his drink. His eyes drifted as a woman walked by the bar. She caught him looking at her, and she sent him a scowl that left no room for interpretation. But, somehow, Cooper managed to double-lift his eyebrows.

"Well, even if Cooper is a scoundrel, at least he showed up," Michael said.

"There's no way Eddy shows up," Patrick said. "He's probably all the way to Seattle by now."

He looked at his pocket watch again. According to his timepiece, Edward would arrive in less than a minute.

"Want to bet on it, cousin?" Patrick asked.

Michael shook his head and waved off his cousin's remark.

And then the door opened. Edward sauntered into Quimby's dressed in a well-tailored three-piece suit and a wide-brimmed fedora. He carried a briefcase full of illicitly earned money and a boisterous attitude that wafted through the bar. There was not a hint of worry on Edward's face.

Michael sank his gaze. He couldn't believe that Edward showed up. He couldn't believe that Edward's pride and narcissism had led him to resume his regular activities.

All things must return to balance, Michael thought.

Edward strolled through the tables and walked directly to Cooper, who reached his hand out to shake Edward's. Placing the briefcase of money discreetly on the ground next to Cooper, Edward looked around the room. His eyes moved over the shadowy booth in the corner without any sense of recognition or caution. He seemed controlled by pride.

Edward looked Cooper in the eye and greeted him as an old business partner, unconcerned with the corruption and violence they had both perpetuated.

Cooper nodded to Edward, and then he turned his attention to the bartender. With a subtle glance, Cooper gave the order.

"Great to see you, Mr. Bishop," Cooper said. "If you'll excuse me, I'll be right back."

The police chief stood and scurried through the crowd, disappearing into a dark hallway.

Edward, thinking nothing of it, rotated on his barstool and faced the mirror behind the bar. He analyzed his face. It looked tired. He smiled at himself, proud of his accomplishments, proud of his rise to the top of the world. Then, he stood to get a better look at himself in the mirror. He straightened his tie, admiring his knot.

The bartender walked to the other side of the back counter and pressed a button, signaling the man below the floor. Edward didn't notice. He had become entranced with his own green eyes in the mirror.

Click. Snap.

The floorboards under Edward disappeared. Gravity carried him unwillingly through the trapdoor. He shouted as he fell, but the sound of the crowd muffled any trace of noise. Michael watched as Edward disappeared into the underworld, into darkness.

No one seemed to notice. Or maybe they didn't care. Maybe this happened all the time around town at places like Quimby's.

Patrick shot the last of his drink and nodded to his cousin. They stood in unison, emerging from the shadows of their corner booth. They walked through the crowd of wooden tables and left Quimby's. As they opened the doors into open air, warm rain fell onto the city streets. Michael watched as the rain ran along the concrete to a steel drain. The rain disappeared underneath the city, invisible.

Epilogue

irds chirped in the tall pine tree; its branches waved in the calm breeze. The sun rose over the Cascades, illuminating the green grass and apple trees around the small, white house. The chill of mid-autumn brought with it a sense of comfort.

Michael enjoyed waking up early these days. It gave him the stillness he needed for his morning ritual of Tai Chi and reading from Mr. Lao's book. He didn't have to be at the docks for another two hours, just a short walk down the street to the river.

After retrieving the newspaper from the concrete driveway, Michael sat on the steps of his front porch. He pulled up his jacket collar to ward off the morning chill.

Opening the newspaper, he scanned the headlines.

Mayor Baker had won his re-election campaign. Calvin Coolidge took the presidential election against John Davis. A woman had even been elected governor in Wyoming.

Michael wondered if he could ever make an impact in city politics. He knew the city's underground, and he had a clear vision for city improvements. And he had a large stash of wealth in his cellar vault that he needed to use for the benefit of others.

The thought evaporated as he turned the page.

The Solomon Band was playing at a nightclub on 3rd Street next week. Maybe he would walk down there and listen. Maybe he could leave a large donation to the band.

On another page, Michael saw another staged photograph of Portland's police force pouring alcohol from a wooden cask into a sewer grate. Michael laughed; he knew Cooper had another barrel underneath the grate to catch the liquor. He wouldn't let all the profit go to waste.

"What's all this laughter about so early in the morning?" Emma said as she joined Michael on the porch. "Did Patrick and Josephine finally make the paper?"

She carried a sleeping baby boy in her arms. The baby rustled as the sunlight hit his face. Michael stood and walked to his wife. He kissed her on the cheek. Emma passed the boy to Michael, who took him comfortably and began to rock as he stood. The porch's floorboards creaked under his shifting weight.

The screen door opened again, slowly this time. Michael's daughter wobbled her way through it and grasped her mother by the leg. Emma picked her up and carried her on her hip.

"What a beautiful little family we've got," Michael said.

Emma smiled at her husband and moved closer to him.

Michael looked out onto his front yard. His eyes began to wander down the street, moving toward the river, which ran beyond the houses and the trees. His thoughts traveled below the concrete, below the road, and into the hollow dirt. He thought he could hear faint echoes reverberating far below.

Afterword

The Shanghai Tunnels are embedded in Portland folklore. As a boy growing up in Northeast Portland, the legend of the Shanghai Tunnels always fascinated me.

As I grew older and developed my studies of history, I began to recognize the blurred lines between the history and legend of the Shanghai Tunnels. Old Town did have an interwoven series of underground tunnels that connected various establishments to the docks along the Willamette River, but some historians doubt the use of the tunnels as a den of vice. Those historians cite evidence that the tunnels were used strictly for legalized transportation of supplies so that people on the streets didn't have to see the supplies being transported on the sidewalks and alleyways.

Other historians, however, cite the lack of written evidence as proof that nefarious activities took place within the tunnels. Trapdoors have been found on bar room floors that lead straight into the tunnels. And legends have to start somewhere, with at least a hint of truth.

Though the use of the tunnels as secret passageways for illicit activities might be in doubt, the act of being "Shanghaied" is not. There is evidence to suggest that young men were kidnapped against their will and sold into slavery onboard vessels; one of the most popular destination for these vessels at the time would have been Shanghai, China.

Portland does have a seriously corrupt past. During Prohibition, high-level officials worked closely with bootleggers to facilitate the movement of alcohol within the city's speakeasy system. Opium dens abounded in the city, as did brothels and gambling houses. While some might have existed within the underground tunnels themselves, most were much more visible. Portland's location on the West Coast, far from Washington, D.C.'s governmental grasp, made Portland an ideal spot for those who wanted to operate illicit activities.

Portland's connection with Shanghai doesn't stop with the tunnels, either. Prior to World War II, Shanghai shared many characteristics with Portland in terms of nefarious activity. Western governments controlled various pieces of Shanghai as they attempted to gain a trading foothold into China's wealth. As a result, the city of Shanghai proved to be nearly lawless when it came to brothels, bars, gambling houses, and opium dens. This made it a perfect place for ships carrying captured American slaves to disappear.

Of course, most of the people who operated these illicit ventures wouldn't have left much written evidence; they wouldn't have wanted to face the legal ramifications for their actions if suspected. So, the written historical evidence for these vice systems are light.

But that doesn't stop the imagination, or the desire to find out what really happened in the underworld of a city like Portland.

Acknowledgments

I want to thank my parents for sparking my interest in Portland's history, and history in general. They pushed me to think creatively, to pursue a desire to share stories. They gave me support to follow whatever path I decided to choose.

Thank you to my wife and children, who give me unconditional love and support as I bounce ideas off of them. Thank you for giving me time to be creative. I love you.

I also want to thank my teachers and writing mentors who have helped me sharpen my skills as a writer and storyteller. Whether you knew it or not, you've had a major impact on my life's path.

And to the people in the city of Portland, who have guided me through my journey through the city from a kid into adulthood. Thank you for shaping my worldview.

About the Author

Tom Malone was born and raised in Portland, Oregon, where he learned to love rain, coffee, and books. He spent time exploring the city, the forest, and the coast. Malone studied journalism and history at the University of Oregon, Spanish at *la Universidad de Oviedo*, and earned his master's degree from the University of Portland.

He has taken dozens of road trips throughout the United States and continues to travel throughout the world. Currently, Malone teaches secondary English near Denver, Colorado, where he camps, fishes, hikes, and snowboards often.

Also by Tom Malone

Portlanders
Portland, Oregon: just another big American city. Tall
buildings, millions of people, systemic problems, and a vibrant
culture. In this collection of fictional short stories, take a walk
through Portland from the perspectives of everyday people.
Everybody experiences the city differently based on their own
lenses, their own backgrounds, and their own motivations; it's
the people who give a city its identity.

World History: A True Story
Explore the story of world history from its beginnings all the
way to the modern day by looking at major civilizations, eras,
people, and cultures that have shaped the world we live in.
This brief overview of world history will spark interest, refresh
learning, and provide a well-rounded look at how the world
has reached its present state.

Across Americana

Ben's plan is unfolding perfectly. He is graduating from college. His dream job is set. Plus, his girlfriend is staying in his hometown and marriage is on the horizon. Then, on his college graduation day, he loses his job offer and his long-term girlfriend. Ben's best friend is leaving for the East Coast at sunrise. With nothing to hold Ben back, he embarks on a spontaneous cross-country road trip to New York City to begin an unforeseeable future. Along the journey, Ben encounters adventures that change his future forever.

Sloan Fitzpatrick: Middle School Journalist

Sloan Fitzpatrick is nervous about his first day of seventh grade. His best friend moved to another state. The school bully grew taller over the summer, while Sloan remained short. Plus, he registered for a Newspaper class just because his crush was the Editor-In-Chief, even though he knew nothing about journalism. After interviewing a city politician for his first assignment, Sloan finds himself wrapped up in the school newspaper. But he also finds himself caught in a political corruption investigation and he's in way over his head. Now, how's he supposed to handle seventh grade?

In the Shadow of the Spanish Sun

Jason embarks on a six-month journey to study abroad in Spain. When he arrives, he knows nothing but his own culture: an environment of greed, spiraling economic standards, and fast-paced rat races. After encounters with immigrant pick-up soccer, exotic cultures, and pushing the limit of fun, Jason dives too deep into these Spanish subcultures. He may find it difficult to return to his life in the United States. Then, he meets a girl. Will love turn him into an expatriate?